Sisters Living in a Man's World

Miss Elspeth's Desire

India 1878

Elspeth Forster, the eldest spinster sister and part owner of Forster Shipping Line, has never known passion. But that's about to change.

After their youngest sister marries, Elspeth and her middle sister Isabelle decide to use their ships for more than just business by taking the adventure of a lifetime. In India she might find a man who can teach her all the things that will keep her warm in her advancing age. But she never expected that an unscheduled stop would put her within Aeddan Fitzsimmon's sights.

Returning from a top-secret mission, English spy, Aeddan Fitzsimmons, finds passage on the *Zephyr*, a vessel in the Forster fleet. From the moment he steps aboard, the statuesque redhead entices him like no other ever has. Now in India he has a new mission: keep the elegant Elspeth safe from those who'd use her connections for their own purposes, while wooing her into his bed.

Miss Isabelle's Craving

Shanghai 1879

After her sister's successful marriage, Isabelle is sure she'll only ever be an old maid aunt. That is until she meets Langdon. He's tall, he's dashing, and he excites her enough to take a walk on the wild side. But with a month to explore Shanghai before her sister and husband have decreed they must return to England, time is short.

Langdon wants Isabelle from the first moment they meet, but with news that she's leaving shortly, he's propelled into action after she makes her proposition.

Marriage is the only answer, but he's got other pressing issues. Hunting down the importers of opium and pressure from his superior to see if the Forster sisters are involved.

Between the opium problem and issues with running Forster Shipping, Isabelle is learning to accept her sexuality and changed circumstances. It's going to make their first weeks of marriage full of adventure and danger.

A Very Merry Widow
England, 1884

Louisa thought she'd made the right choice. Jeremy had been the man she'd loved, but he wasn't who she thought he was. After he dies in a horse riding accident, she wants more. Not another husband, but perhaps a lover who'd fulfilled her needs while she raised her daughters.

Albert never expected to return to England, let alone to take up the family seat or the title of Earl of Conney. Yet here he was, returning from the wilds of Australia, with his friend, Frederick. A convicted felon. He'd sworn to himself if he was going to assume the title, he'd use the influence that went with it to clear his friends name. Brothers-in-law, Langdon Devereaux and Aeddan Fitzsimmons are the connections he needs, and they bring him into the contact with Louisa Lavenwood, a beautiful and aloof widow with two gorgeous but young daughters.

But she has a dark secret, and this unwilling hero feels the need to save her. Along the way passion explodes and they're helplessly lost in its thrall if only they can overcome them, then perhaps more than passion lies in their future.

THE SEARCH SERIES

A VERY MERRY WIDOW

A SEARCH NOVEL

Imogene Nix

PROLOGUE

Louisa watched as the casket containing the body of her husband, Jeremy, was lowered into the ground. His coffin of dark oak and silver fittings shone in the weak daylight, and emotional numbness filled her senses. The fog of the morning had lifted a little, but the cold seeped into her bones as she dragged the heavy, black shawl close around her shaking body. The sounds of weeping from her mother-in-law beside her had been her companion since the accident. Now with the funeral passed, there was only the wake left to survive, then she could consider what came next. Where her future lay.

Her hand, clenched in a black kid glove, was slightly obscured by the black mourning veil she wore as she wiped at her cheek, hoping they'd not look too closely and know. Black would be the only colour she'd wear for a year because convention dictated it, followed by another year of grey, half-mourning. She hated knowing that she would be restricted again.

The bombazine of her gown, heavy and stiff, dragged at her body as her mind whirled with everything and nothing.

Since Jeremy's death, so many emotions had enveloped Louisa, but she'd held them tight within her breast.

Fury that he'd been so stupid as to be riding in a storm.

Grief that the man she'd loved had been taken from her.

But most of all, *betrayal*, because she knew who he'd been with.

There was more, she just knew it, but hadn't yet had time to enquire of her family's man of business. A man like Jeremy, one who'd lied to her face, who'd strayed just days before she gave birth... The truth was coming out, and she welcomed it with a vicious stab of honesty.

A storm was brewing—rage growing—and if *her ladyship* thought she'd simply keep quiet and sweet, she was in for a startling awakening. The roiling fury had grown in the last three days, and she promised herself that soon, she'd release the poison and begin to heal.

As soon as the requirements of widowhood were done, Louisa told herself as her eyes stung.

Exhaustion dragged at her weary mind.

She barely heard the words of the minister, committing her husband's remains to the ground.

All she knew was, with a child and a newborn babe, she was a widow. Alone in a man's world.

A hand reached out, took hers. *Elspeth.* Both her sisters, Isabelle and Elspeth and their husbands had made the trek back to the family home to support her when she needed them most. Men who were well-born. Men who she hoped would protect her from her mother-in-law's vicious tongue. Men who would protect her while she learned what she needed to know and while she decided what her future would look like.

Now wasn't the time to explain. There hadn't been time to do so before the funeral, but once Jeremy's family left, her sisters and brothers-in-law would hear all. It wouldn't be pretty, but she'd need their support. To make plans. Not just for herself but also her daughters.

Dirt was pressed into her hands, and she glanced down at it. "You need to throw it," Elspeth muttered.

She followed the instruction without a word, crouching down to ensure it thudded on the lid of the casket. Then she stayed there for a moment, silently considering. Finally, she rose.

The minister extended his hands. "I'm so very sorry for your loss."

She whispered something. It was probably the right words, but right now, she held tight to her control, the only thing that had bolstered her for the last few days. Ever since learning of Jeremy's betrayal and death.

At the gate, the carriages waited, one for her and her sisters. Their husbands would ride beside the jet-black conveyance. Another waited for Jeremy's grieving parents, and the rest of the family who'd attended had arranged their own transport.

Walking to the vehicle, silence echoed, apart from the cry of a crow. The sound crass and discordant.

Awareness that his family followed was cloying. Freedom was what Louisa craved most right now. Her sisters would surely see that and understand.

It was only once they were settled inside the carriage and it was moving that she took their hands. "Thank you for coming, sisters. We must talk. But after his family leaves." Her voice sounded scratchy from the night before, sobbing into the pillow that still faintly echoed the scent of Jeremy.

"Of course we would come." Isabelle patted her hands.

"You needed us, so we're here," Elspeth offered.

Looking at her sisters, both married with their own children, and returned to England, she wondered if she'd been too young. Too innocent. Too unaware when she'd accepted Jeremy. Thoughts of that day, the gown she'd worn, and the flush of success had gulled her into accepting a flawed man.

Her sisters had been initially concerned but had relented after she'd told them she wanted no one else. They acquiesced and as a young girl of seventeen she'd married Jeremy.

Now at twenty-three, she was a widow in black.

❧

Jeremy's family had finally left as the night drew in. Dinner was quiet in the formal dining room; the staff brought her favourite—a solid and warming meal. The staff, even now, stood with her, protecting her as did her own family. Now, settled around the large fire in the parlour, she would tell them everything.

Isabelle and Elspeth crowded in beside her. Warming her more effectively than the fire could, while their husbands, Aeddan and Langdon, filled the wing chairs. They were strong, reliable men, and the right partners for her sisters, Louisa knew.

"What do you wish to tell us, dearest?" Elspeth gripped her hands.

"He... Jeremy. The night of the accident? He'd been out. There was a tremendous storm which blew in and he ventured home in it. But he'd... He had a mistress, Elspeth. A woman in the neighbouring township. He'd been with her."

Silence descended on the room. "You're sure?" Aeddan leaned forward, imbuing the question with power.

"Yes. I received a note yesterday. Before your arrival." She fished about in the pocket of her gown and drew it out with shaking hands. "Here, read it for yourself."

She didn't wish to ever see it again. The memory imprinted on her mind.

Dear Mrs Lavenwood,

Allow me to offer my condolences. Dearest Jeremy and I were as close as any man and woman could be. He confided in me, prior to the accident, that your recent interesting state and the doting on your daughter were difficult for him. He was a man who needed to be first in everything, including your affections, especially given his unfortunate position at birth.

However, it is my expectation that a token of his regard will be forthcoming to me. My expenses do not end with Jeremy's death as there is a child. As such, I feel it is only right, in light of the closeness we shared, that I should be granted a portion of his fortune, which I understand he personally used to purchase your family home.

I will, of course, be more than willing to engage with your solicitor at a time that is convenient to him.

Lady Pamela Jezerey

Aeddan swore and thrust the paper to Langdon, whose eyes glittered with fury as he read the missive. The paper then was read by both Elspeth and Isabelle.

"He had no claim on the house?" Aeddan queried. "So, he cannot gain any control of the Forster Shipping money or property?"

Elspeth shook her head. "When we drew up the marriage settlement, both Isabelle and I ensured the house did not pass from the family's control, nor any of the business. Louisa was young, and it was the best way we could protect her. The portion that went to Louisa was significant, but was not used in any way for the upkeep of the house or to pay the staff. They were all in the employ of Forster Shipping."

Langdon smiled. "And of course, he duly signed that?"

"Oh yes," Isabelle said with a smile. "We had our man of business bring in a senior solicitor from London to ensure everything was watertight. We love our sister." She shrugged then turned to Louisa. "We wanted to ensure her needs and those of any children were protected."

Aeddan stood and stalked to the fireplace, looked at it for a long moment. "With regards to this child this woman is claiming is your husband's. Has anyone questioned the veracity of her claim? That the child…"

Langdon nodded. "Yes, I agree. We need to establish if indeed the child was Jeremy's."

"No. I don't wish you to do that. Not openly or behind my back." Too many things had occurred, things Louisa knew nothing about until now, and she'd not allow anyone to hide this kind of information from her. Never again.

"But dearest," Elspeth stated, but stilled as Louisa shook her head.

"But you should know, Louisa. If the child *is* his… His parents should take some kind of steps."

Her laugh was discordant. "No, they won't. If this child is his, it's a bastard…" She huffed, because she knew that sounded callous. "I don't know the right answer, but if I've learned anything during this time, it's that his family shies away from truths that do not conform with their norm. Now then, I need to make decisions. Good decisions."

"But the child…" Isabelle leaned in. "It's innocent. It should be protected."

Louisa shook her head. "If there's a child, and I don't know the answer, what if it's not his?"

"Then we find out," answered Langdon. "Once the truth is known, then you can make a decision."

Louisa bit her lip, hearing for the first time the truth in his words. "Find out then," she whispered. "If it's not…"

"You have no responsibility," answered Isabelle.

"Perhaps now is the time to travel up to our properties," Elspeth added. "Take some time away while this is—"

Louisa inhaled deeply, felt the air in her chest, and prepared herself mentally. "Elspeth, much as I would love to run away from all this, you've both sheltered me for far too long. It's time I stood on my own. Took control of my life. I intend to see this through and to become an equal shareholder in Forster Shipping. I have two daughters who need to see their mama as an independent woman, and for too long, I allowed others to direct my life and felt secure in the lack of knowledge. If I've learned nothing else, it's that I'm strong and capable."

Louisa sat upright in the chair and stared forward at first one then the other sister.

When they both opened their mouths to remonstrate, Louisa held up a hand. "No. It's true. I will no longer be passive, sisters. I will see this mess of Jeremy's through, and as for Jezerey, well, whatever you learn will be dealt with by the solicitors. There is a full year of black, then when I can wear other colours. This is the time when I will consider my options."

This new Louisa was merely the tip as plans and ideas were unveiling in her mind. Not yet fully formed, but beginning to cascade. *I need time.* Time to let go of the dream, time to formulate her plan, and time to unravel the threads of a life barely lived before she could decide what and who the new Louisa would be.

"Living here? It's no longer enough, and I will need your support soon. Lady Constance is most insistent I should move to the Hall..." Before her sisters could speak, Louisa held up a hand. "...which I have no intentions of doing. She plans to take control of me and my life and my daughters' lives too. That I will not tolerate. Just as I will not tolerate her waspish friends and their whispers."

"We'll put paid to the biddies, my love," Elspeth answered. "You'll have our unwavering support and those of our circle. All you need to do is ask."

"Good," she said. "Because I've already sent for our man of business and the solicitor from London. I will stand on my own two feet, and I will protect what is mine and ours."

CHAPTER

ONE

Louisa moved in the saddle, uncomfortably aware that today was the first day she could move outside her house in brighter toned clothing. The soft blue of her riding gown, a welcome relief from the two years since the death of her husband. She'd endured the endless-ness of black, before the half-mourning of grey and lavender, but now, she'd thrown that off, though many had counselled her that she should at least employ the use of a widow's cap. Two years of openly grieving for a man who'd duped her in more ways than one had come to an end.

The horse danced beneath her, as if it understood the turmoil that still filled her.

"Come, Lightning," she whispered, patting the side of the horse's neck. "We will only have to stay here for a little longer, then you and I shall have a nice, long gallop through the park."

The carriage swept out of the drive while she watched. Lady Constance had been quite open in her righteous fury at Louisa now embracing the future, one that would take her far from this area and her sphere of power. "I was never going to allow myself to languish," Louisa told Lightning as much as herself. "There is a world out there for Eleanora, Marina, and I to see. And see it, we shall."

She sprang the horse then, feeling the power beneath her as it sprinted forward, over the drive and through the bushes heading for the long park.

Wind caught at her, whipping around, and for the first time, she gave herself fully to the pleasure, leaning low over the horse's neck. If her groom was keeping abreast, she couldn't say, because she focussed on the rhythm, the bunching and releasing of muscles beneath her, and the wind rushing toward her. She chuckled with joy, gripping the reins tight, until the end of the park came in sight, then slowed the horse and turned it before coming to a stop.

The house was hidden from view, and nearby she could hear the ocean, the waves crashing on rocks. It was the life she knew, but was it the only future? What were her choices?

The latest missive from Elspeth urged her to join her sisters for the more relaxed summer season in Bath. The entire haute ton wouldn't be in residence as they would have been previously—to banal for them—but enough would be there that it would be an excellent entrée into society. It wasn't that her sisters enjoyed the endless pleasures, but there, the husbands conducted their work, covert though it may be, in a relaxed atmosphere.

Gripping the reins, Louisa scanned the ocean. She'd barely travelled anywhere, and the sea had been forbidden by the strict aunt who'd come to stay after her mother's death. *I've never really had a lust for travel, so why now am I wishful of such opportunities?* For the last two years, she'd struggled to understand the desire that grew stronger daily.

"I will go to Bath." The girls were now of an age where travelling was possible, especially if she brought a maid and the nursery attendants. She didn't have a lady's maid to concern herself with, since Yates had chosen to retire here, so she would simply engage one there. *Yes, I shall join them, but will insist on taking a house of my own.* "I'll write to Corvings today to make arrangements when I get home, Lightning." A wave of pleasure surged, as if somehow making this decision was the first of a new adventure and potentially a new life.

She turned Lightning's head and sprang the horse once more, on a quick laugh. As the horse moved away from the escarpment in the direction of home, wind whipped at her hair, and she didn't care. The girl who'd been the innocent Louisa was gone, replaced by a woman ready to embrace a new future.

CHAPTER
TWO

Albert Montclair surveyed the land of his youth. England. He'd returned to complete the transfer of his father's property, to visit the grave of his mother, and to finally cut the ties that bound him to this benighted land. Wild emotions surged. It had been over a decade since he'd left, angry at his father, still grieving the loss of his mother.

The ship rolled on the ocean, but after many months at sea he didn't notice it, standing with his legs widely placed. All he could consider was that he was finally within sight of land.

In his cabin sat his trunk, packed with the same exacting fashion as every other aspect of his life which he was able to control. Including the letter that had changed his life yet again.

"We'll be making landfall tonight," muttered his friend and co-traveller Frederick.

"So we shall, my friend," Albert said. "But I wonder what will unfold when we arrive at the Hall?"

Albert didn't miss the wince Frederick gave. A free man finally, Frederick been charged with theft in his teens—a trumped up charge—and Albert's father, as the local magistrate, had decided that Frederick should be indentured for ten years to a local leaving the area as a result. Albert understood Frederick's concerns about being a previously convicted felon in England.

Albert had been a rebellious teen, and as second son, a trial for his father. He himself had been sent off to join the forces as soon as he was old enough. Shipped off before his friend, Frederick's, sentencing, infuriating the powerless Albert. He'd never forgotten it though. It had been pure chance that brought the two childhood friends back together, where he'd 'bought' his indenture but he remained thankful for that turn of fate.

"I'm still not so sure I should have come back," his friend offered.

"You're a free man. And before we return to our homes, I want your name cleared. It was a trumped-up charge—" Albert answered.

"But it's done. I'm free now."

"Exonerated would be better." He turned back, squinting in the sunlight. "Then once I finish my business, and you have the rest of your family sorted, we can return home."

Frederick simply stared at him.

"We've been over this. You've got your own farm, you're ready for a future, and should find a wife," Albert said.

Frederick laughed.

"What?"

"That's truly hilarious, Albert. I should find a wife? You're titled, with land and money. It should be you who's thinking of settling down, making sure there is another generation to uphold the honour of your family name."

Albert understood his friend's point of view, but until the death of his older brother, Thomas, he'd been the second son. The one who wasn't expected to do the succession and impregnation of a wife. He'd never considered his future.

He'd been free to make of himself what he would, and he had.

But since Thomas' death just before his father's nearly twelve-months ago, he'd not bothered to think about such things. Instead, he'd focused on the agricultural property he'd built, initially with Frederick as his overseer, then later he'd assisted Frederick to do the same, with a selection from the government.

Now, Albert was the Earl of Conney, and Lord Cimmaron, with an estate, tenants, and commitments in a country that was no longer his own. His home, while not salubrious, was his. The land, verdant and green, also his. He'd built it with the sweat of his own brow, working right alongside men he trusted.

"I have a cousin who can take responsibility for the family name and the next generation," Albert said, sure that he could pass off the responsibility he neither wanted nor had ever desired.

Frederick simply shook his head, and Albert was uncomfortably aware why. He might tell himself he didn't want the responsibility, but ignoring it was a whole different thing. He was now the head of the family. It was Albert's responsibility, ensuring the tenants' needs were addressed, the house was being kept and... His mind strayed to thoughts of Alicia. The girl he'd told himself had been his future all those years ago. A willowy girl with fine blonde hair and grey-blue eyes.

Realistically, it was unlikely she was still at home with her parents, unmarried and waiting for him. It wasn't like he'd had her at the forefront of his mind for the fifteen years he'd been absent from England. She'd been fourteen and him almost eighteen. Neither old enough to declare anything. Now, she'd be twenty-eight or twenty-nine. Well past marriageable age, and likely with a growing family.

He opened his mouth and closed it again, because what was there for him to say? He'd meet with his man of business in London. Learn what he needed to know, then make decisions. Until he understood how things sat, he could make no further decisions. Instead, he simply turned back to view the outline of the place where he'd need to unravel his unwelcome inheritance.

L ouisa inspected the walls of the house Corvings had arranged for her household with satisfaction.

"It's close to the centre of town, though I'd have felt better if you'd have stayed with one of us," Elspeth said.

"Perhaps, but I'm independent now, Elspeth. I need somewhere to feel like I can sit quietly alone."

Elspeth started at her words, and Louisa reached out and took her sister's hand in her own.

"I'm not ungrateful for all the assistance you and Isabelle have given me," Louisa said. "I do, however, need to stand on my own. I've daughters to raise, and…"

"You need to make a life for yourself. We do understand, dearest. It's just that we both feel this responsibility," Isabelle offered. "However, you should be more than comfortable here. There's enough room for you to be able to host soirees. Elspeth and I will be here to guide you, should you wish it, and you'll have access to society. Agatha Pensworthy is hosting a ball next Friday, and she has already promised me invitations. I'll ask her to send one for you as well."

Louisa knew Agatha Pensworthy's events were considered a social highlight. As the newly minted Duchess of St. Croix, she held an almost unassailable place in society. As the cousin of Elspeth's husband, they could call upon family connections to assist Louisa's entry into society.

"We could all travel together, Isabelle. What do you say, Louisa?" Elspeth urged.

Excitement gathered. The only balls she'd previously attended had been local gatherings of the gentry. "I'll need gowns—"

"Madame Celestine has already arrived from London, and I have fittings tomorrow. If you agree to my plan, arrive say around ten. I know that's most unfashionable, but I can then arrange for her to bring an assistant. We'll refurbish your wardrobe, so you're prepared until a new wardrobe can be delivered."

Louisa nearly blushed but understood that to gain acceptance by society she'd need to look the part as well. "Yes. You're absolutely right," she whispered, suddenly feeling a little out of her depth. Before this, she'd been more than happy to make do with the work of her maid and the local seamstress, but if she truly wished to move in society, then she'd have to continue to change herself, her mindset and—

"Dearest, forgive me, but as you've not been in society previously, should we engage a dance tutor for you?" Elspeth enquired.

"Oh... I hadn't considered that," she answered.

Isabelle nodded. "Unless you don't wish to dance?"

Once more, Louisa squeezed her sister's hand. "It's a ball. My first society ball. I may be a widow, but I will dance. Unless that's considered *declasse*?" she queried.

"Not at all. But you must be cautious with whom you dance, my love. You don't wish to be considered fast. That would indeed be ruinous," Elspeth offered.

"Indeed, I shall need your advice and guidance. I'm woefully uneducated in the ways of the nobility and society. At home, I knew who and what, but it was all local. Here, I'm unprepared." Biting her lip, Louisa understood, both her sisters were now firmly entrenched in the society she wished to move. Without them, there would be little chance she'd be welcomed, and neither would her daughters when the time came. "I'll need a maid too," she added.

"We will see what can be arranged, but that may be trickier here than in London. There just aren't as many experienced lady's maids in Brighton these days," Elspeth explained.

"We'll help you, my dearest. We love you and our beautiful nieces, and we want you to be happy. Now come. We should head back to the hotel and plan for you to transfer to your house in the morning," Isabelle soothed, and Louisa nodded. "And once everyone is settled, we'll arrange for the children to visit with your two. They're positively bursting with excitement to see them again!"

She cast a single last look at the red brick house and smiled. Lady

Constance had been most seriously displeased when she'd announced her intention of staying for the summer in Brighton, but Louisa had embraced the opportunity. She'd use it to launch herself into society, for the benefit of her daughters.

I will control my life. I will be happy.

CHAPTER

THREE

LONDON

Albert heard the rattle of carriages, the call of voices, and the noise before he stepped foot outside the hotel foyer. Alien. Every sound discordant.

"We certainly aren't at home," murmured Frederick.

"No. That we are not." And that wasn't something that made Albert feel overjoyed. In fact, he'd only been on English soil for three days and he already yearned to be back aboard a vessel, sailing away from the foreign shores he could no longer call home. Instead of comfortable pants and a shirt, he was restricted by a suit, jacket, and ridiculous hat, cravat, and even a bloody walking stick!

Today he would meet with the family's man of business, Emile Corvings. He'd taken over some two years previously and had been the one who'd made contact in the sparse correspondence which had taken so many months to reach Albert.

Before leaving the building, the concierge stilled him. "Sirs, will you be requiring a carriage?"

Albert blinked at the man dressed in the livery of the hotel. "Uh, no. Frederick and I shall walk."

"Very good, sirs." The man bowed low and opened the door for him, and Albert and Frederick stepped out into the weak sunlight.

The hubbub of the crowd grew larger and more cloying. For a moment Albert stilled. Too long in the service of his majesty, and then later in what was called 'the bush' to be comfortable in this situation. He inhaled deeply, waiting for the nerves in his hands and throat to cease jumping.

"This direction, I believe," Albert said, and they walked slowly away from the building.

"It feels discomforting to be visiting a man of business. I mean, it doesn't feel all that long ago that I was in a prison, then sold... indentured and on my way to hard labour," Frederick said, breaking through the fog enveloping Albert.

"Indeed. However, we need to petition for your exoneration—" Albert stated.

"If we can find someone to corroborate my innocence. It's been nearly fifteen years, Albert. I doubt..." He sighed. "You seem to see the title of 'freed man' as more of a problem than I do. All I want to do is see my family. Find out if there's some way to assist them, and if they wish, bring them home with us. I've plenty of room and can fund them now that I have a good income." Frederick spoke slowly, and Albert understood his friend's pain.

"I requested Corvings to make enquiries. Hopefully when we arrive, he'll have news about your sister and mother and where they are. What they're doing, and if there's a way to help them."

Frederick simply grunted, then they were once more silent. As they crossed a busy intersection, carriages moved quickly back and forth around them, then they stepped onto a paved sidewalk and continued their walk. A large, grey stone building loomed, the brass plate on the door gleamed and the copper number *seventeen* shone against the red paint.

"This should be it," Albert announced.

The heavy knocker thudded against the plate at Albert's move, and the door opened. "Sirs?" the man within queried. He looked like a glorified manservant, and yet this wasn't a private house. As surprising as the façade was, Albert refused to allow anyone to see how it affected him.

"Albert Montclair and Frederick Hollis for Corvings." He handed over one of his newly made cards to the man, who peered at it, nodded, then opened the door wider.

"Of course, my lord. Please come in," the manservant said, shuffling out of the way.

A cold breeze tickled the back of Albert's neck as he stepped inside and handed his hat over silently and Frederick did the same.

"Please, come this way, my lord." The procession of three made their way down a cold, dark corridor before stopping at a door with a brass plate proclaiming *Emile Corvings, Esq.* The door was opened by the manservant and both Albert and Frederick were ushered inside. "Mr Corvings? His Lordship, The Earl of Conney, and Mr Frederick Hollis to see you."

The man behind the large, wooden desk rose. Of a middle age, he was trim, with keen blue eyes hidden beneath gold-rimmed glasses. "Sir, it's good that you finally arrived. Please take a seat, and of course Mr Hollis too. We have much to discuss." He turned and pulled a large leather tome, then a second from the shelves.

They settled into the seats, but before they could begin, Corvings rang a small, silver bell and requested tea.

BRIGHTON

A missive lay on the salver and Louisa eyed it with suspicion. The embossing denoted it was from the family man of business, Corvings. Her sisters had traditionally met with the man since he'd taken to handling their business, but now Louisa felt as if she too could and should participate in the decision making. However, this time, she would enquire as to the finer details of her financial standing. As a widow, with daughters to raise, she needed to ascertain exactly what lifestyle she could commit to, and what she could provide for her children.

"Isabelle and Elspeth have been meeting with him for years, but..." She bit her lip, aware that her sisters were more forward and experienced in this realm. Able to make decisions for themselves. For the first time, she'd be standing on her own two feet.

Of course, before his death, Jeremy had received regular updates from the man, but she'd never been privy to them. Even after his death, Isabelle and Elspeth and their husbands had taken on the duty of clearing through his desk. But now, settled in Brighton and ready to establish herself in society, she felt, if not capable, then at least ready to consider the mess they'd had to deal with.

With shaking fingers, she reached for the parchment, raised it, and broke the seal.

My dear Mrs Lavenwood,
I received your enquiries and am more than happy to provide you
with the information requested. However, due to the amount of
explanation that may be involved, I would humbly suggest that I
call upon you, on Thursday next at ten in the morning, to make
such explanations. I trust this will meet with your agreement.
Should this not, then please apprise me by return express and I
shall endeavour to call upon you at a suitable time.
Your servant,
Emile Corvings, Esq.

She carried the letter over to the sofa and sank back down. The amount of explanation? What could that mean? *Maybe I should ask Elspeth or Isabelle?* For a moment, she wavered, before straightening her spine. "No. I have to do this myself. I cannot and will not rely on my sisters for the rest of my life." But it was difficult when they were her chief support systems. The only ones she could really turn to.

Long moments passed as she held the letter in her hands and stared at the door. Emotions tumbled inside her, fear warred with elation, and she allowed herself to feel all of them, because it reinforced that she was making decisions for herself.

Inhaling once, then again deeply, Louisa took a moment to centre herself before rising with a nod. "Thursday next will be fine." She hurried to her escritoire, snatched up a sheet of paper, her pen, and ink to reply.

Dear Mr Corvings,
Thursday next is suitable to me. I have relocated to the house you procured for me in Montpelier Crescent, Brighton.
I await your arrival.
Louisa Lavenwood

Satisfied, Louisa folded the parchment and slid it into an envelope, then scrawled the address and cleared the desk before rising. Today, she was meeting with the dressmaker and modiste, then the shoemaker would be given directions for boots and slippers.

"It's really happening. I'm taking control of my life and setting course for the benefit of the girls." She felt lighter than she had for so long, even as the distant wail of a child filled the air. Next, she would look for a governess, one who would empower her daughters. Preferably someone who'd stay with her until the youngest was ready to make her come out.

Biting her lip, she began to write a mental list.

Meet with Corvings.

Engage a governess.

Find a professional dresser.

No doubt the list would grow, but this was a beginning.

Feeling prepared, she headed for the hallway. "Drammers? Call for my carriage please, and I'll have my cape. Tell the cook I should be back for a late luncheon, then I'll go up to the nursery. Thank you."

The butler, who her sister Isabelle had lent her, nodded his head. "Very well, madam." With a click of his heels, he disappeared.

Louisa stepped into the parlor. It was small but perfectly proportioned, and she wondered if the pale cream wallpaper would suit the house overlooking the water, before disregarding that. Perhaps it was time to relocate from the family home, rather than renovate. Then she'd be free of the memories and the whispers of a society who knew her husband and the truths she wanted to shield her daughters from.

The young housemaid, Millie, stepped into the room. "Mister Drammers sent me with your cape, ma'am, and he said the carriage would be here in an instant. The boys in the stables had it ready and waiting."

"Thank you, Millie. I appreciate knowing what's happening."

"Yes, ma'am," she said and handed the cape over.

Louisa slid it around her shoulders and fastened the deep green frogs at her throat before smiling at the girl. She was pretty enough, and capable. Perhaps when she made her decision about relocating to London fulltime, the girl might be enticed to come with her? It would be good to have a younger set of servants. Youngsters closer to her age, who may understand her needs. Louisa made a mental note to watch the girl to see if she'd suit her in the longer term, although from what she'd seen in the last few days in the house, she was certainly capable and pleasant.

Drammers appeared in the doorway. "Your carriage, madam," he said in his very correct, deep voice, and added a bow.

As she followed him to the door, Louisa smiled, feeling a level of satisfaction that had been missing in the last few years. Her life was changing, bit by bit.

Albert peered out the carriage. This trip to Brighton was a pain he could best do without, but needs must, and he mentally shrugged his shoulders. He'd had no intentions of travelling here, but Corvings had insisted he meet with the viscount, as he'd indicated the man had the connections necessary to get Frederick's case reviewed. *That is the vital aspect. Frederick must be a free man.* Only then could his friend be assured that any woman he may choose for his life partner would be a true choice, not a matter of settling.

Glancing in Frederick's direction, Albert wondered about what went on in his friend's mind. Did he too wonder about the vagaries of life? Did he feel the injustice of choices removed as Albert did?

The years Albert had spent serving against his will bit deep. It wasn't that he actively fought against his fate, but he'd suffered in being removed from his mother and the loss of the girl he'd once planned would be his wife. He'd grieved the inability to assist Frederick, his close, true friend, in his time of need. "Not this time," he muttered.

"Albert?" Frederick queried from the other side of the carriage.

"Just thinking out loud," he answered. To be honest, he was having difficulties reintegrating into English society, and more than once he'd muttered something aloud that he'd meant to keep inside his head. Too many years among the rough and tumble, he thought.

He turned back to the window, watching as the lush green paddocks passed by.

CHAPTER

FOUR

Another ordinary morning passed. One without the claims of Louisa's deceased husband's family. She leisurely paraded down the promenade beside the beach, feeling the breeze on her face, the scent of salt in the air. It was lovely and restful, but somehow not quite what she wanted, needed, or even expected.

"Dear, you don't seem to be happy." Isabelle stopped her with a gentle hand on her arm.

Louisa bit her lip. "I don't know what it is, but I feel at a loss, sister. I will be meeting with Corvings in the morning, but there is an..." She looked to the ocean for inspiration. "I'm missing something, and I don't know what it is. This is restful, but I want to do something with my life. I'm not like you and Elspeth. You went out there and lived in a world only men can own. I'm not... I'm not adventurous. I'm the sister who stayed home, married, and had babies. But inside me, I feel empty. Hollow. I adore my children, but I want..."

"More?" Isabelle offered with a raised eyebrow.

"Yes. More." She couldn't look at her sister. She didn't want her to know just how deep the well of yearning was. After all, she should be happy. She'd escaped the cloying arms of Lady Constance, and as for Pamela Jezerey … well, Corvings and her sisters' husbands had dealt with her. Now that the period of mourning had expired, she'd thought the freedom would be just what she needed, whereas it now seemed it was only a step along some journey she couldn't see an end to.

"Dearest, you're the only one who can understand what it is you want. Elspeth and I? We're more like Father. You tend to be more like Mother, but you barely knew her, which is a shame. You want your children and home, and we know you like security. Certainty. But that life is gone, and what you have is changing, like you. Whatever it is that you need, only you can make it happen. Only you can chart the voyage into the unknown and set the course. But you need to know what you want." Isabelle stopped for a moment and so did Louisa. Isabelle held up a hand and ticked off, "Love? Security? Freedom? Adventure? Experience? Each one will affect your path. Each one has its own map."

"But Aunt—"

"Our dear, long-departed aunt was a harridan. She refused to allow you any of the freedoms Elspeth and I enjoyed. Yes, she cared for you well, but you were young. She was the one who stopped any of us having our season, and she was the reason you never had the opportunities to be and do. Let us not forget, she was the one who encouraged your marriage in the first place, only she didn't live to see it happen or what came next." Isabelle sighed and shook her head. "I shouldn't have spoken like that. She meant well."

For the first time in years, Louisa didn't remonstrate, instead she examined her older sister's words in her mind. "It is true she felt none of us would benefit from a season, but I had forgotten all the times she planned to be where Jeremy was. She always meant well."

Isabelle inclined her head. "Perhaps she did, but the results are still the same." The children—both hers and her sister's in their prams pushed by the families' nannies—caught up to them, and

Louisa watched as her sister reached out to the oldest of her brood. "I hear there is a new business selling ices at the end of the promenade. We should try one."

Understanding that her sister didn't wish to discuss any of their personal business in front of the nannies, Louisa nodded. "Well, if that's the case, we'd best hurry along, in case they run out." The group set off for the end of the promenade, but with every step, Louisa considered Isabelle's words, seeking guidance from them.

A pleasant hour was passed, with Louisa and Isabelle tasting the ices, while the children were given smaller pastry delicacies before they headed for home. They may have talked during the interlude, but Louisa only half-attended.

Farewelling her sister, her children, and nanny when they reached her door, Louisa and the nanny ushered the children into the hallway of the house, and Louisa handed over her cape.

"Mama! I'm not feeling well," Eleanora, her older child, whined, and Louisa looked to the nanny.

"I'll take her up to the nursery, ma'am, and get her settled. I'm sure she'll be right in no time." Nanny nodded, taking Marina in her arms and leading Eleanora up the first flight of stairs.

"I'll come up later, once luncheon is cleared, to check on her. Go with Nanny, darling." Louisa called as she watched them climb the stairs, then a footman slid forward, silently raising the older girl-child in his arms and carrying her out of view.

Louisa sighed and wandered into the salon, looking at the bright green walls. It was the only room bar the nursery to be covered in this paper, and she had to admit, it probably also was the reason she barely used it. It was dark and dim, cloying, and she never felt quite at ease in the room.

The footman cleared his throat, and she turned. "Yes?"

"Perhaps the doctor should be called for Miss Eleanora. She's been unwell for the last week or two. Also, Cook asked if she should serve lunch in the next hour, and maybe send a baked custard up for the children?"

Louisa nodded. "Of course. Let's serve then, and yes, something soft and easy to digest for Eleanora. As for the doctor, do you know of one?"

"Indeed, ma'am. I believe Dr Justice has been retained by Mr Corvings. We can send for him," the footman offered.

"Yes, please send for him. Let me know when he will arrive, and I will attend the nursery."

He bowed and withdrew from the room, and Louisa turned, wondering what could be wrong. Eleanora wasn't a sickly child; indeed, she'd best be described as a rambunctious and active girl. The bane of Nanny's life. So, what could possibly ail the child?

lbert seethed. Corvings had sent him yet another missive.

Sir,

I regret that another client requires immediate assistance. I will call upon you on Monday next to discuss the situation at length. I trust this delay does not inconvenience you.

Your servant,

Corvings

Another delay. And now, just to rub salt into the wound, there were *cards*! Invitations to banal assemblies and luncheons. Someone had tattled that he was in town and the society members who still frequented Bath had figured out who he was and where he was staying.

The door behind him opened, and Albert turned to see Frederick enter the room. "What's that?" His friend indicated to the salver.

"Invitations." Albert couldn't control the sour note in his voice.

"Invitations?" Frederick grabbed a plate and selected from the dishes a mixture of ham, eggs, and kippers, before retreating to the table. "Sounds like fun. Where are we going?"

Albert spun to look at his friend. "We're not. I'm not accepting any of them."

Frederick stopped, knife and fork still suspended in the air. "Why not?"

"They're society do's. I don't... We can't..." Albert shook his head.

Frederick stared at him. "Why not? You're an Earl. Eligible, if not exactly rolling in the cash."

"I've no interest—"

"It could be fun, Albert. I mean, imagine you taking me, an ex-indentured servant and prankster, with you. We might meet some ladies. At the very least, it might liven up our time while your man does whatever it is he's doing. And you might even get to meet the mysterious judge who signed off on everything."

Albert couldn't believe what he was hearing. At least, not for a moment, and then a seed of devilry took root. *Why not indeed?* He was invited. Society in England no longer had a claim on him, so what did he care what they perceived once they saw the man he'd become? After his estate was settled, and he'd made plans, he'd leave the benighted shores and likely never again return. *Nothing to lose.*

"Nothing to lose, perhaps you're right," he said quietly, before scanning Frederick. "We'll need to visit a tailor. Neither of us have suitable attire."

His friend goggled. "I was merely joking."

"But I'm not. Eat up and I'll look through this stack and see if anything appeals, then we can arrange fittings for both of us."

Frederick's mouth remained open.

"I'm not going if you're not, so eat up man," Albert told his friend.

Indeed, he considered that this might just be the best way to pass the time while waiting for Corvings. He'd never been the kind of man who'd sit back and wait for things to happen. Too much experience had taught him that the leaf upon the breeze got swept away like so much detritus.

He grabbed ham and eggs, avoiding the customary kippers, and settled at the table with his friend. The house they'd rented was situated opposite the sea and he allowed it to soothe him while he and Frederick ate in silence.

When they were done, he rose. "I'll be down shortly. We'll visit the tailor then perhaps a walk along the boardwalk."

Frederick grimaced. "We don't have to—"

"We don't have to do anything we don't wish to do, but idleness doesn't sit well. We have three days until Corvings will attend us, so I plan to use the time. I'm also... We should acquire some horses too. I feel we should visit the house, if briefly. I wish to see the conditions for myself before meeting with Corvings."

His friend nodded and they both withdrew.

A fine tremor began under Albert's skin. Something he couldn't explain beyond feeling that finally, he was taking steps to control the situation. Making decisions and preparing to make the most of his future. His future with only himself in control.

He climbed the stairs to his chamber.

Louisa hugged her arms around herself, desperate for someone... anyone... to support her. But there wasn't anyone else. Her husband was dead and that she no longer mourned. Her sisters would come if she asked, but... *I'm a grown woman.*

The physician hovered over the child, tutting and shaking his head, while Eleanora simply lay on the bed, pale and breathless.

This was the third episode this week, and each time Eleanora became a little less of herself and more of a shadow. *A wraith.*

Dr Justice rose from the bed and turned, looking around the room, before stilling and looking at the wall. "Madam, we should speak outside." His voice was gruff and set the butterflies in her belly soaring again.

She nodded and followed him to the door, but not before she glanced back at her daughter. Eleanora's eyes fluttered closed, and she slid a hand to Nanny. "Care for her. I'll return soon."

Once the door was closed, she indicated to the doctor they should descend the stairs. If the news was bad, she had no wish that Eleanora would hear before Louisa herself had come to terms with it.

Within the parlor, with the door closed, Louisa slumped into a chair. "Please. My daughter?"

"Is being poisoned, madam." The harsh tone slammed into her, and it took a moment for her to discern the meaning of the words.

"Poisoned?"

"The wallpaper, madam. I've been reading reports of that particular type of paper. The green, vivid, and unnatural colour contains arsenic. Your child is breathing it in daily. Her sister...?"

"I... They each have their own rooms." She pushed a hand to her stomach, willing for a moment for the wild fluttering to cease. "But how?"

"Many used that paper, and it poisons slowly, breathing into the system and the toxicity slowly kills those in direct contact with the paper."

Louisa stood up, spun, marched to the wall, and pointed. "This paper?"

Dr Justice nodded at her curt demand. "Indeed. You must relocate immediately, if you have any hope of ensuring the health and well-being of yourself and the children."

Louisa stared at him. "Relocate. I..." Her mind spun before she realised, she needed Corvings to make arrangements. Until then... "I will contact my sisters, and we will vacate as soon as I can arrange it. Eleanora... She'll not suffer greatly if we move her?"

"Madam, to stay here will only exacerbate the illness. Every minute she breathes in the fumes, increases the chances of her death." His censorious tone hammered like spikes in to her brain.

"Thank you, Doctor. I'll have my man contact you." She turned away for a moment before whirling back, her mind making a split-second decision. "I should like, for the duration of our time here, to continue our professional association." At the man's nod, she exhaled. "Thank you for your time, Doctor Justice."

The grizzled man gave a small nod, but as his hand settled on the knob of the door, he turned back. "Your decision and the immediate action will set you both right."

She bit her lip and watched him leave, slumping into the chair. In truth, the headache she'd been battling for the last few days now made sense. Taking a moment to regroup, she stood, made her way to the escritoire in the corner of the room, and settled to pen a missive, first to each of her sisters, then to Corvings.

Next, Louisa rang the bell and the butler opened and peered within. "You rang, madam?"

"I did. I need these sent immediately to my sisters, and this one," she said, waving it, "to my man, Corvings. I believe he's in town. Then make arrangements for the household to relocate to a hotel. You might consider enquiring as to a suite at the Grand Brighton? Also make arrangements for the staff, until such time as an alternative house can be leased. Then give orders for the house to be packed in preparation."

He stared at her. "Madam?"

Louisa stared at him then realised he would not be aware of the intelligence the doctor had just given her. "The house is decorated with arsenic wallpaper. We must immediately vacate it. Miss Eleanora is very ill already. Poisoned."

The man blanched but nodded. "Indeed. I shall attend to your directions immediately."

Once the door closed, she rose, tottered to the chair. "What have I done?" she muttered. Her first decision as an independent woman had brought about the near death of her child, how could she possibly be sure that the second wouldn't make things worse? She worried her lip. "Is this what it's like for woman living alone and making decisions for themselves?" That terrified her.

She'd been sheltered and allowed herself to rely on others, and now, when she'd finally made a stand for herself, the outcome hadn't been a success. Was that because her reasoning was flawed?

Her hand rose to dash away the hot tear forming. "I'm going to fix this. My decisions will be better." They simply had to be.

CHAPTER

FIVE

The day was bright and warm, and Albert and Frederick had finished with the tailor, leaving with the promise that new suits and shirts, together with the necessary underwear, would be delivered in batches in the next few days. They'd also ordered canes, umbrellas, hats, and shoes to ensure that their entrée into society would cause no ripples. Neither he nor Frederick would be embarrassed he determined.

Of course, Frederick had decried the costs, but Albert was well-able to support them both, given the way his personal enterprises had taken off. It seemed that wool was indeed a necessary and even desired commodity, and he was reaping the benefits, as was his friend.

"We should head to the hotel for lunch, Albert, before we make the necessary enquiries concerning mounts. You should send a message to the man you know to arrange—"

"I like the way your mind works, Fred. This afternoon we'll arrange for horses to be made available to us. And on the morrow, I believe we should ride out to the house, and determine the situation.

Surprise them, if you will. I plan to bring back the books for perusal," Albert announced.

Frederick grinned.

Albert was pleased with what they'd achieved during the day.

"I thought you planned...?" Frederick's brow rose.

Albert shrugged at Frederick's words. "Not tomorrow. Once the clothing arrives, we enter society with a splash, eh?"

Frederick groaned. "I'd really rather not. I don't know one fork from the other and..."

"*Pshaw!*" Albert said. "If that's your greatest concern, we can arrange a private tutorial to assist."

Frederick looked unconvinced and swiped at his hair. "I don't have the breeding," he said with gritted teeth.

Albert snorted. "I might have the breeding, but I was never prepared for this position. We'll sink or swim together." Of course, he wasn't unaware of Frederick's concerns, but the bravado he feigned was the only thing making this whole jaunt bearable.

They rounded the corner of the building and looked at the scene before them. Three carriages had pulled up and a woman climbed down from the first one, followed by a tall man carrying a child in his arms, swathed in a blanket, before another woman emerged, carrying a smaller child.

The majordomo pushed the doors open wide to accommodate them and a couple dismounting from a second carriage while the third disgorged what was obviously the servants amid a flurry of portmanteaux and trunks.

"I wonder what the story is," Frederick said. "I see there's some high emotion, but the child in the blanket looks ill."

"Indeed," answered Albert. "Perhaps later today we might enquire and find out the details." Not that he was overly engaged with the situation. Children and families and intrigues were, for now, beyond his interest. His mind was elsewhere, focussed on what he needed to achieve before they returned to their adopted homeland.

The woman carrying the smaller child handed her to what he was sure was the nanny, and Albert watched as she tottered and nearly fell. Of his own volition he moved, extended a hand to support the woman.

"Thank you, sir," she murmured and glanced up. The blue of her eyes and the beautiful bow of her lips catching him unaware, and he stared, like a transfixed fool.

Frederick made a noise, as if clearing his throat, and Albert realised he'd become statue-like. "I beg your pardon," he said and released her.

With a small nod she moved away, up the few steps and into the building.

"Albert?" Frederick's voice echoed in his mind.

"Yes, we should go in," he muttered, hoping to avoid questions until he once again regained both his composure and his wits. But the visage of the pale woman with the golden blonde hair haunted him. *Who is she? What is her story?* They were questions that spun in his brain, and, from experience, he knew would continue to do so until such time as he'd learned everything there was to know.

Frederick nudged him again, and Albert entered the hotel, noting that the staff were fluttering around the man who acted protectively toward the woman carrying the child. The woman with the golden hair.

"I'll find out who she is," Frederick said as he opened the door to the dining room.

Albert trailed behind him. "What?"

"You're staring, friend. I doubt that's somewhat acceptable even in your level of society."

Albert heard the surprise in Frederick's words, and he swivelled as the doors shut behind him. "I... It's nothing." Not that it was, he allowed privately, but he had no intentions of allowing himself to be beguiled by a beautiful woman.

He followed his friend and settled in a chair beside him, pleased they'd had the forethought to arrange a table for the lunch appointment. But it was with a fractured mind that he made his way through the meal.

§♠

Louisa hovered in the doorway, noting that Nanny was settling Eleanora into the bed. The child smiled weakly, and Louisa couldn't help but inwardly castigate herself. If only she'd been aware. Her sisters and brothers-in-law waited in the next room, in a small sitting area. In the end, they'd taken two full suites to accommodate the family, ensuring Eleanora wouldn't need to share a nursery while still so ill.

"Ma'am, I'm sure she'll be alright soon. Now, I'll send down to the kitchens for a broth for Miss Eleanora, then when she's feeling a little more the thing, I'll have them send up a nice, soft pudding. Nothing like a bit of sweets to raise the spirits, eh poppet?"

The little girl nodded slowly, and Louisa sighed. "I'll go check on..."

"Yes, ma'am. The tweeny will call me if she needs assistance with the little one. But you should go, get a bite yourself and rest." The older woman's gaze had narrowed on Louisa's face, and she was thankful Nanny didn't say what she was clearly thinking. That she looked a little peaked herself.

"Then I'll go and—" She dipped down to pop a tiny, soft kiss on Eleanora's cheek before making her exit from the room.

Elspeth hovered by the door. "Is she settled?"

"Yes, thank you, sister." Her voice wasn't much above a whisper, aware that her ill daughter lay just beyond the sitting room.

"You mustn't reproach yourself, my love. Corvings likely took the house based on the referral from the agent, and—"

Louisa shook her head. "No, I should have known, when I saw the wallpapers. It should have occurred—"

"Nonsense," her brother-in-law, Langdon, corrected. "You've been in mourning for two years and learning about these things wasn't a high priority for any of us. And at least the physician was aware enough to make the determination in time for everyone to recover. Now, I would recommend that you settle in and make yourself comfortable until Corvings is able to secure you another residence."

"I'm not sure…." Louisa allowed herself to sink into one of the overstuffed chairs and wiped a shaking hand over her brow. "Perhaps I should return to the house."

Elspeth sank down, the skirts of her gown billowing around her. "Is that really what you want, Louisa? To return to the house and have to deal with Lady—"

Louisa bit her lip and a single tear slid down her cheek. "No, but for the children…"

"Louisa, you must make decisions for you. The children will be fine. They will accept your decisions, but you must be firm. Decide exactly what it is you want."

"I did that before, Elspeth. I married the man I thought I knew, and look how that turned out. Then moving here, I nearly brought ruin down on my head. Eleanora is sick because—"

"Nonsense," said Aeddan. "You cannot control how the owners have disregarded advice regarding the furnishings of their home. Neither can your marriage be something you wallow in." His tone was harsh.

On a gasp Louisa sat up in the chair. "Wallow?"

Aeddan smiled, lines near his eyes crinkling. "Well, that worked better than planned," he muttered. "But yes, you've been in the doldrums since relocating to Bath. I would humbly suggest that we pass the season then return to London, feeling ready to tackle it face-on. You need time to make the transition, and that's what this was about. You won't manage it if you continue to tell yourself that your decision-making is flawed. Now, Elspeth and I must away. I have a meeting, and Elspeth should rest."

Louisa turned back to her sister. "Rest? Are you ill… or…" A seed of understanding exploded. "You're increasing again?"

Elspeth smiled and nodded. "Yes. But don't worry about me. Simply decide what you want. Isabelle and I will always support whatever choices you make. Just make them for you, not because of the past, or because you think it's what society expects. Isabelle and I decided to go our own way and that gave us the chance to be who we wanted and to achieve a life we barely thought possible for ourselves. You're still young, and there's time for more, my love."

Louisa waited as Elspeth and Aeddan left the room and considered both their directives. *Decide for yourself. Don't wallow.*

She'd made the decision to leave the house where she'd been born and raised. Where she'd settled as a young bride and had birthed her own children. Yes, there'd been a misstep, but perhaps Aeddan was right? Perhaps she'd been so busy questioning her every decision that she was too afraid to jump.

Confusion swelled inside her. What to do? She'd wanted to be the one in control. She needed to prove to herself that she could do it. Perhaps instead of calling on her sisters and their husbands this time, she could have done it alone, but she hadn't. The support had been welcome, but she could have done this by herself. Perhaps that was the first step in taking control. Make the decision without asking or needing their agreement.

"I can do this. I'm capable of making decisions for myself." The words sounded so strong, but was she able to carry that out?

A knock echoed, and she sat up in the chair. "Yes?"

A young maid entered the room and bobbed a curtsey before extending her hand with a letter. "Madam, we've received a letter from Mr Corvings directed from your previous residence. Also, given it's luncheon, would you rather a meal in the dining room or a tray sent up?"

An easy decision. "I'll take a tray in here today, thank you. Also, a pot of tea."

The girl bobbed again and withdrew from the room. Louisa rose and headed to the lush bedroom. Her maid had already completed the clearing away of her clothing, and the headache she'd been fighting swelled.

"I'll eat then have a bath, I think." She could be happy with that simple decision, then perhaps she might lie down for a while. Let her head settle, then she'd be better able to consider what else she should do.

Louisa laid the letter on the dressing table. She'd peruse it after she'd eaten. Then she drifted back to the sitting room to await the breaking of her fast.

Albert settled his aching rump in the saddle. It had been long months since he'd ridden, and a side glance at Frederick told him his friend was also uncomfortable. "Nearly there, Fred. Another mile or so and we should come upon the fence line."

The road was pitted and in poor condition, and he frowned, aware that while they'd not yet reached the edge of the property, the hedgerows had seen little care. The neighbouring house had always worked with the estate manager to ensure that the boundaries were well cared for, but what he was seeing flew in the face of everything he remembered.

They travelled in near silence, and he noted soon enough when they came across the marker of the change of properties. The hedgerows now were in serious disrepair. Brambles snaked onto the road, and limbs of overhanging oaks littered the gaps.

Albert turned to Frederick. "I don't know what's been happening."

"Or not," his friend agreed. They came upon the main gates, locked with a large chain, and Albert dismounted.

Albert passed the reins over with a "Hold her, would you?" then made his way to the gate and peered within. The drive was shadowed and also overgrown. His hand slid through the metal of the gate and waved. "Hello! Anyone here?"

A grizzled man, bent almost double and looking nearly a century old, shuffled out. "How you, and watcha want?" Then he stilled, straightened slightly. "Master Albert?"

It was the old stablemaster, French. "Yes, it's me, French, and Frederick Hollis. Open up, would you?"

French nodded and reached into his pocket. "A sight for sore eyes you is. Never thought nowt more could happen to surprise me." He slid the key into the lock, and it crunched open. French then unwound the chain. "I were told not to let anyone in. I reckon though, it's right that I open it for you."

Frederick dismounted and together they led the horses through the now open gateway.

"Who gave you that order, French?" Albert enquired.

"Mr Storck, the manager. He said no one was to come in," French answered, the tone of his voice dripping with disdain. "He said even if the master came, it should be directed to him first."

Albert frowned at the directive. "Indeed? Well, he's in for a sore surprise then. Fred and I will ride up to the house, but before we do, give me some details as to what's been happening. The hedgerows and fences—"

"Aye. Storck didn't want us spending time on those things, but to my mind, he's taking advantage of no master, he's all but living in the house, and my missus, you remember Jessup, your mother's maid? She said the servants are being directed to give him access to the main rooms. Things are disappearing, items of value, and anyone who questions is being turned off. The house isn't being cared for properly as there is now only two housemaids and all bar the senior footman, Venning, have been cast off."

None of French's words improved Albert's state of mind. "Right, then gather up anyone you feel might be concerned and bring them to the house. We'll go up ahead."

French's eyes drew together in a frown. "Sir, with all due respect, you are armed?"

Albert inhaled. "No."

"I am," muttered Frederick.

Albert glanced at his friend.

"I felt a degree of discomfort based on the little I'd heard, so thought it prudent to be prepared," Frederick explained.

"You'd heard?" Albert wondered at his friend's comment.

"I have had some contact. My sister and all..." Frederick shrugged.

Albert nodded and the two men once more mounted their horses, then with a gentle move he touched the sides, and the horse moved forward into a trot. They made their way up the drive, and every metre reinforced Albert's disquiet.

The house rose from the greenery, its visage mouldy and lichen-covered, the drive itself strewn with weeds, and Albert wanted to snarl. He remembered the days of his grandfather, with the immaculate presentation of the house and entryway, only eighteen years before.

He realised now, that when his father took control, the care of the house itself had decreased. Even the last time he was here, not long after Frederick's arrest, the situation had declined. But this? It was a shambles.

"Your father and brother saw the property as little more than an opportunity to raise funds for lining their pockets," Frederick said.

"You didn't tell me." Albert didn't miss the bitterness in his voice, but right now he didn't care. Had Frederick duped him? Was he in some way... No! Frederick was his friend. "Why didn't you tell me this?"

Frederick sighed. "How? What good would it do you? Before-hand, you were never going to be the one in charge, the one who made the decisions. And later ..." He shrugged. "It just would have upset you. I thought it best you come into this without any precon-ceived ideas of what you'd find. But seeing the state of the hedgerows and hearing old French, I thought you'd best know at least what was likely ahead."

Albert seethed, but on an unemotional level he understood that Frederick's words really wouldn't have made any appreciable difference, except maybe he'd have come here earlier.

They stopped the horses at the front and dismounted. A boy of maybe thirteen or fourteen scuttled out, his eyes large and round. "Ye best not stop here, misters. Ain't going to get in if Mr Storck has anything ta say about it."

Frederick cleared his throat. "This is—"

"Who the devil are you, and what are you doing in my home?" a booming voice echoed.

The boy shrank back, and Albert looked up. A spare man, with a harsh face, whiskered and decked out in the dress of his father, if he didn't miss his guess, was on the top step.

"I'm guessing you're Storck?" Albert drawled.

"Aye, and this is my home," the man blustered, shifting his weight from one leg to the other.

Albert let a tight grin escape. He was going to take Storck down a peg or two. "Really? And you're Conney?" He kept his tone even.

"I don't have to answer to you. Now get off my property." Storck flung out a hand, and Albert had to supress a spurt of laughter.

The sound of crunching footsteps behind him alerted him to the presence of French and his men. It emboldened him to make the next announcement. "Now that may be slightly difficult. Since *I'm* the Earl of Conney and you're on my land, I believe it's you who should be vacating *my* home."

The man's eyes widened. "You're lying. Melkhurst, get rid of—"

"Well now, Storck. You're being a mite hasty," drawled French just as a huge man lumbered through the doorway and onto the step behind Storck.

Albert knew Melkhurst. Not bright, but burly, he'd been a brawler in his younger years, and was some three or four years older than himself. "Melkhurst, so you're still here? I thought you'd have made your fortune with your fists in London by now."

The man in question stilled, then tugged his cap from his head. "My lord. Tis good to see you back where you belong. I see—"

"Melkhurst, I said—" Storck began.

"Ain't doing no bidding for you, Storck. This here is the Earl, and he's the one who'll be giving the orders now," Melkhurst answered.

Storck's face took on a crimson tone. "I said get rid of…"

"That's enough," Albert called. "This is my home, and I want you out. Now. Melkhurst, would you be good enough to show Storck to the gate."

Melkhurst nodded. Not that Albert was under any illusions. After all, if Melkhurst had been working with Storck, there was history, and likely the man wouldn't be reliable enough for tasks that required integrity. But right now, Albert needed someone with muscles.

Storck whirled, hands balling, and he reached for Melkhurst, who dodged and grabbed the older man around the waist.

"Let go of me, you fecking oaf!"

Melkhurst ignored Storck's yells and lifted him off the ground and started striding up the drive, French diving in behind him, gleefully calling out, "I've the keys, Melkhurst."

"Check his pockets before you close them," called Frederick, and Albert found himself nodding. "He may have other keys, and we'll need them all."

Louisa woke slowly, her eyes taking in the surroundings of the room in the suite. Her head didn't ache quite so badly, and for the first time since she'd relocated to Brighton, she felt in control.

"Perhaps the physician was right when he said things would improve." Louisa hated the weakness of mind she'd been experiencing over the last few weeks. She'd been wanting to take control of her life ever since Jeremy's death, but once she'd arrived it felt like every bit of willpower had eroded.

"Today I will send a message to my sisters. I will arrange a rental property. Once that is settled, I will seek a dance tutor for myself." Just saying the words aloud gave her a feeling of accomplishment.

Ringing the bell, she sent for the maid and directed her to find her cream gown with rose patterns. The material was cheery, if not quite the pink of fashion. Louisa sat at her toilette table, and Millie dressed her hair, chattering that "Miss Eleanora looks brighter this morning. Nanny said she's already eaten toast and drunk some warm milk. Nanny also said if she were feeling better, she might take the girls to the park for some air."

"Tell Nanny I'll pop in to check on Eleanora later. I have some appointments I wish to make and perhaps then I might see if my sisters are available and pay a visit to the milliner. I'd like to purchase some bonnets for the girls and myself. Something that will suit the new wardrobe I'm planning to order."

"Yes, ma'am." As the woman's hands worked with her hair Louisa closed her eyes, allowing the soft touches to relax the last of the pressure in her skull. There was something soothing about Millie's moves, and she'd nearly drifted off when the maid said, "All done, ma'am."

Louisa opened her eyes and smiled, reaching up to touch the elaborate, curling design of her hair. "That's lovely, Millie. I should send you to spend more time with my sisters' dressers if that's what they've taught you so far."

The woman smiled and a tinge of pink highlighted the apples of her cheeks. "Thank you, ma'am. Uh, I also have something that came for you via courier this morning." Now her eyes sobered as she reached into the pocket of her gown.

"Oh, from who?"

"Lady Jezerey." The words were whispered but they had the effect of plunging the whole of Louisa into a chill.

"When did this come?" Louisa enquired.

"Senningham said it arrived at the hall two days ago. They were unsure initially, but he directed that you should see it. Said keeping those secrets would only make it worse. Miss Louisa, you should let your brothers-in-law deal with it," Millie pleaded.

"No. Hand it over."

The maid did so, but not before Louisa caught sight of her distress. She wanted to tell Millie it was nothing, but the words... the *lie* wouldn't come. Anything Pamela Jezerey had to say could only be malicious and carefully curated to ensure that Louisa paid. The woman had spent the last two years demanding money and favour, and while Aeddan and Langdon had both been towers of strength, it was time for Louisa to stand on her own.

She broke the wafer and read.

Louisa,

I have been most patient, but I am past that now. Your husband, Jeremy, was father to my daughter, Caroline, no matter what lies you've been told. Until now my husband had turned a blind eye to that fact, but I find myself in a position where funding her is no longer the purview of my husband. Jeremy was her father, and Jeremy's estate shall pay. Either you fulfill the bargain he made with me to pay for the upbringing of the child or I will ensure everyone knows your husband is her father and made no provision. Furthermore, I will ensure you and your daughters names are dragged through the mud, as not just knowing but refusing to assist.

My patience is at an end.

P

The words were bitter and cutting. Oh, she knew Lady Pamela and her husband were estranged, and that a child had been borne during their union. Whether or not Jeremy was Caroline's father really wasn't her concern, though both Aeddan and Langdon insisted she could not be. That the woman threatened both her and her daughters, to smear their names, left her incensed!

"Miss Louisa?"

Louisa scrunched the missive into a ball. "It's nothing I cannot deal with, Millie. Now go see Nanny while I write two letters quickly, then I think I will head downstairs to the dining room and break my fast." She tried hard to inject a modicum of gaiety into her words, but she could tell they sounded forced, and Millie's deep frown in reaction reinforced that knowledge.

Once she was alone, Louisa stashed the letter in her pocket and moved to the small writing table and penned an invitation to both sisters. By the time Millie returned she'd closed them and written the direction on the front.

"Have these sent immediately to my sisters," Louisa said. "And once I return, I'll require a carriage."

Millie dropped into a low curtsey and Louisa left the room, heading to the corridor and down to the steps which led to the dining room.

It was mostly silent, and Louisa was thankful, ordering a plate of toast and tea. Her hunger had fled reading the letter, but she refused to let that woman rule her life any further.

❧

Albert scowled as he scanned the figures listed in the books. They'd returned after a brief tour of the house. It was as poor as he'd expected. None of the rooms, bar the master's, had been kept up, and a swift view of the master room led him to think that Storck had indeed decided he was now master of all he surveyed.

He also met with the few men French had hurriedly rounded up, and they all told similar stories of how work on the tenant farms hadn't been done. That they'd had resources swallowed up and that Storck had been redirecting funds from the estate.

Melkhurst returned, and for now Albert believed it better to keep him close even though French remonstrated. "But he was helping Storck!"

"I'm aware of that, French, but right now, keeping him close will allow us to keep an eye on him."

"Then surely you'll stay and—"

"Not today. I'll be returning to Brighton. I have business I need to conduct, but should anything happen, such as Storck returning, you should let me know." He gave the address of his rented accommodation, thankful his grandfather had been forward thinking enough to ensure the children of the estate were properly educated.

CHAPTER

SIX

Louisa perused the invitations piled on the salver. "I'll need to consider which is the most advantageous," she muttered.

Elspeth and Isabelle waited quietly, as if understanding that their sister had to begin to take charge, but she could feel the fine vibrations in the air, as if controlling their need to assist was only just tamped down.

"I know you want to guide me, but Lady Wishart's soiree might be fun," she said.

"Lady Wishart is a rogue, but very nice. You could do worse than associating with her," Isabelle offered.

"Yes, but did you receive an invitation to the opera? That will be the highlight of the social season here," growled Elspeth.

Louisa shuffled through the cards. "Oh, yes."

"Maybe you should attend both," said Isabelle. "They are on the same night, but it is possible."

"That would be a slight... I don't know why they do this. Two events on the same evening. I suppose we could attend Lady Wishart until just prior to—"

"One, Elspeth," called Aeddan. "Remember you're—"

"Darling, I'm expecting, not dying." There was a layer of emotion behind the words, and Louisa's stomach cramped, because in reality who would take on a widow with two children of her own? Her time for romance and love had passed. It was a sobering thought.

Isabelle's hand curled around hers as if the younger sister understood her thoughts.

"Your time will come again, Louisa. This time he'll be committed to you," Isabelle whispered so their sister wouldn't hear, but Elspeth did and gave a knowing nod, and Louisa blushed.

"Oh, hang it, I didn't mean to upset you, Louisa," Elspeth murmured, keeping her voice low.

"No, I had my opportunity, and look at what I did. Now then, let's focus on the invitations. Which one?"

"Oh dear, well, if we attend Lady Wishart's event, then we may not make the opera. But Lady Wishart does have the most interesting people," said Elspeth.

"And her card room is always useful for meeting people," added Aeddan, proving he was still invested in the conversation. Louisa truly liked both her brothers-in-law, but she couldn't help but privately wish she'd met someone like him well before she'd agreed to marry Jeremy. Her life wouldn't now be so difficult. No dealing with the witch Jezerey.

"Louisa?" enquired Isabelle.

"It's nothing. Just wool-gathering. Fine then, now I just need to settle on an ensemble."

Both sisters weighed in, and before long the acceptance was sent out and Louisa's maid was given instructions on what she would wear the following night at Lady Wishart's soiree.

"Have you managed to find acceptable lodging yet?" She hadn't heard Aeddan approach but now he came and settled himself next to Elspeth on a lounge.

"Not yet. I haven't been in touch with Corvings yet—"

"I know of a house. It's by the water. There's no arsenical wallpaper, and it's available immediately. I believe there's room for servants and it has a large nursery." He leaned back. "It may suit. I could arrange for you to inspect it if you like, or I can arrange—"

Tears pricked Louisa's eyes. She hadn't asked and she knew his efforts were an attempt to make her life easier. Aeddan and Langdon were truly caring men. Both of her sisters had married well. She also knew they worked for the crown in some way, her sisters having advised her not to ask too many questions, but she didn't care, because whenever they'd been needed, they'd been there, not just for her sisters, but also for her.

On a whim, she nodded. "I'm happy if you've made enquiries. If you could enter the negotiations for the time we're here."

"Excellent. Now, the other thing, your carriage isn't in the best of conditions," Aeddan started.

"I know. I've already given Billings instructions to seek out a replacement."

He inclined his head. "I know of a lady in reduced circumstances. Her carriage would be an adequate replacement."

Louisa looked at him. "You know of a lady?"

He cleared his throat. "She's my cousin, and her husband died three months ago. She's in straitened circumstances with a small son, and as head of the family, I made certain overtures, wishing to assist her financially. She refused but indicated if I knew someone..."

"Amelia?" queried Elspeth. "But you didn't say—"

"She asked me not to, my love. She's very proud, Louisa, but she and her son are in a most precarious situation. I had thought to offer her a role in the household, and take Daniel, her son, in as well. He could be educated with our daughters..."

"Oh Aeddan, you're a good man." Louisa reached out to squeeze his hands.

"Don't tell others that. It's a... weakness in my line of work."

Alone in the world. In straitened circumstances. That would be so very hard. Louisa blinked. There but for the grace of God... "Aeddan, what's Amelia like? And you say she has a son, Daniel, how old is he?"

Aeddan looked at her. "I've known Amelia all my life. Her father was the vicar at our local church, and she married young. Michael was a charming rogue, but when he died, he'd lost all the money his father had left. Amelia's family had died, her brother at sea and her parents only years before. Daniel must be three or four. I don't rightly remember."

"Would she be open to a position as companion?"

Elspeth and Isabelle both sat up. "You're not old enough to need —" Elspeth muttered, clearly outraged.

"You mustn't settle like an older woman, Louisa," scolded Isabelle.

She smiled at both her sisters. "I'm not. But there's times I'd appreciate someone with me. To talk to. To share concerns with. You're both the best sisters any woman might want, but you also have your husbands and your lives. I refuse to burden you forever, and this way, I can assist another woman. Daniel and Amelia, if they suit, would be welcome. I'll already need a tutor for the girls, so he could be in the school room with them. I think that would suit quite admirably. Aeddan?"

"I could send for them both, if you're sure, Louisa. It's an admirable thing you're suggesting." Aeddan smiled.

"Well, I'd appreciate meeting her first, then we can settle on details." Louisa felt as if a weight had been lifted from her shoulders. Another woman to share the highs and lows. Someone who understood the fears of a widow. To help someone else. The opportunity was one she wouldn't ignore.

Albert spent yet another night perusing the account books, but the more he read, the more he understood the precarious nature of the household and the estate. To do more than simply plug the gaps would mean he'd have to remain in England for longer than it took to clear his friend's name.

It might take years.

That was sobering.

But he had a responsibility. He was the Earl, after all. People relied on him to ensure that the minimal funds still available were invested wisely, that the tenants' needs were addressed, and that the house was restored to its previous glory.

The light sputtered and Frederick rose. "Is it really as bad as you say?"

"Aye. If I can call together a thousand pounds, I'll be doing well, but the property cannot be sold, because of the entailment. Anything that can be, already has been used to pay my father and brother's debts. Though it's clear they were extreme, they appear to have been dealt with by Corvings. There's much work to be done though. The farms, from what I read in the letters from the tenant farmers, are in poor condition. Roofs that need rethatching, fencing fallen into disrepair. The few cattle left are old and should be replaced with fresh bloodlines. It's a sorry situation, my friend. The thing is..."

Frederick nodded. "It will all take time, and you need people who are able to be trusted to oversee both here and at home."

Albert groaned. "I wanted to be going home. I miss the heat, and sounds. I miss the olives of the landscape, and here, everything just feels alien." On a smile, he added, "And that sounds almost poetic."

Frederick sat opposite him. "What will you do?"

He shrugged. "I don't know. I have responsibilities. Ones that I can't just ignore, much as I want to."

"And the property?" Frederick asked.

"I have a good overseer. I can leave him there in the short term. He's honest and reliable. But you—"

"I can give you a month, maybe two, but I will need to go home. There's not much here to hold me. I want to see my sister and mother and bring them home with me if they'll come." Frederick turned to stare at the fire. "Here, I'm still a nobody. It doesn't matter that I have land, I'm not well-born. I'll never be someone, and I don't want to live like that anymore."

Albert understood his friend's position. "If they don't want to go with you, I'll look after them. They'll always have a home, Fred. But I must stay, as it would seem being an absent landlord isn't going to work at this point. I'm going to have to make a plan for being able to direct both properties."

"But it takes months to travel!"

Albert shook his head. "No, Fred. I've read how the new steamships make the journey faster, and they can arrive in a month or six weeks. That will make the travel easier." He sighed. "Not that I want to lose months at sea, but at least it's not like the three months we remember."

Or I could just sign over the property and stay. I'd have a comfortable life as the Earl. I could enter society...

"But are steamships safe? I mean, you're putting your life in the hands of..." Fred's voice trailed away.

It was true, ships still foundered and were lost at sea, but what option was there? "Let me think about it, Fred. But for now, I need to finish running these numbers. Get an idea of how bad things really are."

Frederick rose. "A drink then, and I'll leave you to it."

Albert looked down at the columns of spidery figures. He'd need to know if there were any holdings elsewhere, peruse the will, and meet with the solicitors. He'd purposely wanted to talk to Corvings first, but this was becoming ever more sensitive. A glass was handed to him, and he accepted it with a "thanks." It seemed that no matter which way he considered the issue, it would come back to the same outcome.

"Fred? Thanks." Albert meant it. Without his friend to assist him navigating this quagmire, he'd have struggled by himself.

"It's been my pleasure, Albert. Now, I'll bid you goodnight."

The door closed but returning to the figures was proving difficult. Instead, scenarios rolled around in Albert's mind, and he stared at the fire and nursed his brandy.

Louisa smoothed down the bodice of the gown. "I like this very much, madame. The cut—"

"Makes the most of madame's assets, if you will," the seamstress offered while Elspeth and Isabelle both nodded.

"The material makes your skin glow, Louisa," Elspeth enthused.

"Yes. I like it very much. You had some other materials, you said?"

Madame clapped her hands, and the three eager assistants each brought a range of materials from sapphire blue, through to a rich emerald green, and a brilliant gold and black shot with silver. "Each of the materials should be addressed individually, *non*? This," she said as she fingered the black, "will make an evening gown that even her majesty will find *tres bon*!"

"Indeed. I'll take all the suggested gowns, but I'll need at least three evening gowns and a ball gown with all due speed. Walking gowns, tea gowns, and three habits as well."

"Very good, madame." The seamstress' smile grew wider. "Coats and wraps, gloves and..."

"Yes." Louisa nodded. "A full wardrobe."

Her sisters smiled. "We're so pleased you like the works madame has created for you. She has filled my closets most effectively, prior to each Season. We get exactly the same gowns and styles as the mavens of fashion, but at a fraction of the price," murmured Isabelle.

"Money may not be an issue for us, but we wouldn't have much if we squandered what we do have," Elspeth explained.

"And of course, the silks and brocades you've managed to acquire for me have ensured we've been able to style you so well, ladies," madame offered.

Louisa was surprised. "Silks and brocades?"

"I found the silks in India while I was there... When I met Aeddan," and Elspeth smiled.

"The brocades were something we sourced in China. Even though we left hurriedly, I was still able to find suppliers," added Isabelle.

For the first time, Louisa understood her sisters *had* made a difference. They'd found suppliers that helped to buoy the company while she'd sat at home. It felt... ridiculous and weak. Was that what she'd been all those years?

Jeremy had never really wanted her involved, and in her youth, it seemed so far removed from what she'd wanted to be. She'd yearned to be a mother and a wife, both of which she'd been, but had there been opportunities for her to be more? Perhaps. Maybe that was why she now felt at a loose end. Previously her days had been meeting with the household staff, seeing to the children, and meeting Jeremy's needs.

She bit her lip. "They are truly beautiful fabrics."

"And madame will wear them well. Now come, we'll unpin you and you may dress again."

Louisa waited as the women bustled around, unpinning and removing the cut fabrics, and assisted her to dress in silence. *I will be more.*

Now all she needed to do was decide on the how.

CHAPTER
SEVEN

lbert fumed. He'd sent for the solicitor, and while the man would arrive tomorrow, he felt as if he needed to finalise everything immediately. "My entire life is consumed with dealing with this bloody mess!"

He paced from one end of the room to the other. Stilling at the front window, he noted movement in the house next door. It wasn't overly large, but he knew it too was a rented property. Three coaches drew to a stop, and he waited. Three women were disgorged. The first a beautiful silvery blonde-haired woman, followed by a statuesque, dark-haired vixen. When the third alighted, his breath caught. The woman he'd seen by the hotel.

The second carriage carried two children and what appeared to be maids. Both children were carried, the older appearing still unwell, but not the pasty white he'd caught sight of previously. The third carriage contained servants and baggage. Trunks and valises, portmanteaux and baskets of varied shapes and sizes.

"Fred?" he called his friend to the window. "Look here. The woman from the hotel is moving in next door."

His friend rose and joined him by the window. "Indeed. I'm sure

Sproggs will find out everything in short order. Including her name," Frederick chuckled.

No men. Interesting. There had been a man last time. Perhaps he was a family member or associated to one of the women. Were they all moving into the property? No, there wouldn't be enough rooms. Though his house was larger, there were only three main bedrooms and several for servants. They weren't big dwellings, and three women, children, and servants would be bursting at the seams.

His interest piqued, he reached for the bell beside the window, and when Sproggs entered the room, he nodded to the carriages. "Someone is moving in today next door? Do you know anything?"

The manservant nodded. "Yes, sir. A lady widow and her two children. There is also another woman, yet to arrive with a child, who is supposed to be her companion. The women with her are her sisters. The Viscountess Traughton, and Lady Isabelle Langdon. Both very highly thought of in society. Mrs Lavenwood has two young daughters."

"A fount of information, Sproggs," chuckled Frederick.

"Indeed, sir, I make it my business to know who will be residing next to this house. The owner has connections to the Forster family, which the ladies come from, and Forster Shipping Company's concerns."

Even Albert knew the name Forster Shipping. It was a large, family-held concern, and he'd heard that the female owners were in control of the business. If the woman moving next door was one of the sisters...

"Thank you, Sproggs. Could you please have Cook prepare lunch for us," Albert directed, and Sproggs left the room.

"Forster Shipping. That's a very large business, and if they're the sisters in charge, then..."

"They're powerful. Traughton... Does that name seem familiar," Albert murmured. He knew it, but why? Frustration coursed once again, and this time he recognised the need to control it. To get himself in rein once again.

"Indeed. But I don't know how or why." Frederick's face screwed up, and he shifted in his chair. "It's important is all I'm able to say with any certainty."

"Indeed." Albert settled at the small, round table once more with the correspondence. "The solicitor will be here before Corvings."

"I understand that's not quite what you wanted but—"

The sound of a rap on the door had Albert sitting up, but the portico was obscured, so he waited for Sproggs to enter, after voices had filtered from the hall. "Mr Corvings, sir."

***

Louisa smiled as she scanned the small parlour. It was decorated in tones of cream and mossy green. The wallpaper of figured silk, with deep chairs and highly polished dark woods. The room was comfortable and welcoming. The fire in the grate dancing and jumping.

She turned in a circle. "It is delightful. Thank you, Elspeth and Isabelle."

"The rooms upstairs are also comfortably furnished. The nursery has two bedrooms and Nanny's room," Elspeth added.

"And the family bedrooms are comfortable. They aren't quite as spacious as the hall, but decorated in very pretty peach tones for the second room and the same cream and mossy green as in here in the main bedchamber."

Louisa stilled, gaze settling on first one sister then the other. "You've already inspected it?"

Elspeth blushed. "We wanted to ensure it was right. No arsenical wallpaper and that the rooms were proportioned enough that you'd be comfortable."

Louisa released the tense muscles in her arms. "You were ensuring I'd be comfortable?"

Isabelle cleared her throat. "The last house made you and Eleanora quite ill. Don't think we didn't have an awareness. It was because we suggested the house, because of its size and location, that you took it. We felt we'd done you a disservice."

Unable to contain the nod, Louisa settled into the chair. "You were kind, and I'm being ungrateful."

"Not at all," Elspeth answered. "We know you want to stand up and be in charge. We didn't stop to think that we might be treading on your toes. Please forgive us."

Louisa released a sigh. "No, I understand entirely, and I am grateful. Thank you. Now tell me more about the nursery."

Isabelle smiled, and her face was once again sunny. "It's quite large. Two bedrooms, one larger than the other, and Nanny is settling the girls into the larger room. There's a range of toys, including a rocking horse and blocks, and a warm fire."

"Nanny has her own small room, and there's a rocking chair and child-sized table and chairs, so they can take their tea up there. And a small garden with metal fencing, but it has views of the sea, as does the main bedroom. The same colours as in here too."

"Then I shall be most comfortable. But tell me, when does Amelia arrive? I find myself looking forward to having company in the house."

Elspeth smiled. "She should be here later today, according to Aeddan. He says she's happy to have an opportunity, and her little boy is quiet, but also excited."

"I find myself looking forward to another woman in the house. I think when we reach London, I'll look for a governess for the children, and I'm sure Amelia will be able to assist me in the search—"

"Already? But Eleanora is only four... five. Surely, she's too young?" exclaimed Isabelle.

"Not really. I want my daughters to be well-educated. You both had governesses and opportunities, and I..." Louisa stopped and scrunched her fingers together.

"Aunt Mary was very strict." Elspeth nodded, her curls shining in the light filtering through the windows. "We had time with Father away from the home, and you want to be sure that's not how your daughters are raised."

Inhaling, Louisa took a moment to think before answering. "Aunt

Mary was kind in her own way, but restrictive. I want my daughters to have the opportunities that will expand their choices." Before anyone could speak again, Louisa reached and took the bell in her hands. "Sit down, sisters, and I'll ring for tea. I know Drammers and Millie have been in the kitchen long enough to give Cook some directions." She smiled. "Then we can inspect the rooms and prepare for Amelia's arrival."

It wasn't long after the tea arrived that a knock came at the parlour door. Voices, a child and a woman, could be heard, and Louisa rose, fumbling in her excitement. The door opened and a small woman of a similar age entered the room, bobbing a curtsey while encouraging her little boy to step forward.

"Madam, this is—"

"It's fine, Drammers. Send for Nanny and another teacup if you would. Have Millie stay up there and maybe see if there's some cake for the children? I'm sure Daniel and Eleanora would like that?"

The door shut, and Louisa indicated the chair beside her. "Come sit down, Amelia and Daniel. Make yourselves comfortable."

The little woman, a mousy twig with pale violet eyes and light brown hair escaping from beneath her dowdy hat, nodded. "Thank you, Mrs—"

Louisa already decided that she'd be perfect. "My name is Louisa, Amelia, and I'm sure we're going to rub along just perfectly."

The woman smiled shyly, and Louisa couldn't contain her grin. When the door opened and Nanny bustled inside, she felt a warm glow. "Ah, Nanny. This is Daniel, who will also be your charge. Miss Amelia and I will have tea, but I've asked for Millie to take up some cake, and if you could introduce the children?"

Nanny smiled. "Yes, Miss Louisa. I'll have young Daniel's bags brought up."

"We only have a valise between us," whispered Amelia.

Louisa frowned. "Where are the rest of your things?"

Amelia blushed deeply, and Louisa had a pained understanding they had little.

"Not to worry, Nanny will ferret out what he needs," Louisa said.

Amelia reached over to her son and assured him he should leave with Nanny, and at the same time Isabelle and Elspeth rose. "We should leave you two to get to know each other, but if either of you requires anything..." Isabelle offered.

"I'm sure we'll be fine. Tomorrow morning, I think we should take a short stroll along the boardwalk and make arrangements for the next few days," Louisa answered.

Amelia almost vibrated beside her, and Louisa wondered if she was uncertain of her new role or something else. *I'll get to the bottom of it.*

Once everyone departed, the tea was poured and a small platter of sandwiches delivered to the parlour, Louisa settled herself opposite Amelia. "Now, I want to know all about you. I'm sure you're tired, but if we square this away first, then we can find a routine that suits us all."

Amelia opened her mouth and burst into tears.

"Your Grace, I apologise for the surprise visit. I was supposed to meet with Mrs Lavenwood, but she's relocated, and I need to find her new direction, so I felt today I should step in, and we could begin to sort through the mess of the estate. Have you met with your solicitor yet?"

Albert slid the leather-bound books across the table. "No, I meet with him tomorrow. I did, however, visit the house, and I learned the steward had moved in. He's been milking the books for every penny..."

Corvings sighed and rubbed his brow. "Your brother and father refused to allow me access to the books. I counselled them in the many problems that we would face going forward, but they had no intentions of listening. I suppose I should be grateful they kept me on." Sarcasm laced his words, and Albert frowned.

"Then how did you—"

"Tradesmen would send the bills to me, and I would forward them, with strongly worded letters to ensure payment. Your brother and father were known gamesters, and while they would infrequently do well, they were never keen to part with funds to keep the estate afloat. However, I do have one bright spot. Your mother's dowry was tied, by her father in consultation with your grandfather, and there is a secondary inheritance that was due to come to you upon your thirtieth birthday. A small manor in Cornwall, which has been very carefully stewarded. Your brother and father were unable to access any funds from it, and it's worth a tidy sum."

Albert sat up straighter in his chair, his mind whirling with the knowledge that perhaps he could—

"I would counsel you against using those funds to prop up the estate. While they are significant, there are many years of neglect to the house itself and it will require rehabilitation. You should also visit it to meet with the tenants. Since your mother's death there has been no real interest, your father and brother not having any claim to it, they refused to act in the best interests of the property holder, namely you."

"What?" He rose and scrubbed his hands through his hair. "I don't…"

"I wrote to the last direction your father furnished, and to be honest, had quite forgotten it until you arrived in town. Then it took me some time to peruse the papers. I had to be sure of the values and descriptions before I raised it with you." From the leather satchel, he pulled a sheaf of papers and a large ledger of deep wine red. "Your holdings are a manor house, with tenant farmers. A dairy is also located within the holdings of the manor, and supplies the outlying townships. The property is well-funded, and raises two thousand pounds a year in cattle sales, and there is also a thriving business in slate extraction."

"I guess that means we'll be travelling to Cornwall soon?" quipped Frederick.

"I suppose so," Albert agreed, "but before that, I need to meet the solicitor."

"Well, would you like me to formally accept the responsibility for your books, and will you be taking up residence at the estate?" Corvings queried.

Albert felt as if a large stone sat on his chest. "I'm... As yet, I'm undecided. I have holdings in Australia and must return..." He swallowed, feeling his Adam's apple bob. "But I also have a responsibility to the estate." The sense of helplessness he'd tried so hard to push aside returned. *I should be in control of my future, what I want is tied up with what I must do.*

"You must decide what best complies with your abilities, sir. However, I would respectfully suggest that for the foreseeable future you should place someone in charge of your other holdings, while you address the issues here."

"I have already made plans, but won't be able to remain in this limbo indefinitely," Albert replied.

"I understand that, sir. Now, onto the second major request, that of Mr Frederick's reputation. I have made enquiries, and I feel that we could petition the Viscount Traughton. He has numerous contacts who would be able to assist in this matter."

Frederick laughed. "That's where we know the name from!"

"I beg your pardon." Corvings settled back in the seat.

"Next door! Viscountess Traughton is the sister of Albert's new neighbour. I don't remember her name but—"

"Mrs Lavenwood? She's now next door? How... convenient. Then when I leave, I shall pay a call on her." Corvings smiled, lines crinkling around his eyes. "But for now, let me peruse the books you've given me."

Albert rose and collected the sheaf of papers he'd worked on while looking over the books. "If these figures are in any way correct, the estate is close to sunk," he said as he dropped them before Corvings.

The man scanned them. "Yes, I'd agree. So now we need a plan, one to raise the funds, but tell me what you saw."

L ouisa let the woman sob, understanding all too well that while others might label it hysterical, it was a necessary emotion. When the jag finished, Louisa offered the other woman a handkerchief and rang for more tea.

"Do you wish to talk about it?"

Amelia dabbed at her swollen eyes. "I loved my husband. He was good, but he… money was a weakness. He rather liked to gamble, so once his employer was aware, he would drop extra coin to the house. For the child, he'd say. He was a good man. But after my husband died, there was nothing more he could do. He allowed us to stay in the house, but we couldn't really afford the rent. I took in washing and mended, but the little I had saved was almost gone when Aeddan, my distant cousin, suggested I might be a suitable companion for a younger widowed lady. That my son would also be welcomed…" There was a hint of desperation in her tone. "Please…"

Louisa patted her hand. "I wouldn't countenance you not bringing your son, Amelia, and I'm sure we'll do well. Now then, I think we should talk about your wardrobe. As my companion, you'll be in society with me. You'll need appropriate clothing. I think we should start with a dozen gowns, and I'll request the seamstress come here. How does that sound?"

"But I don't wish to be a burden," and the young woman paled.

"It's not. It's no different to a maid's uniform or a butler's suit. I won't expect you to be shabby beside me, and since I'm arranging new clothes for my daughters, I will arrange your son's as well."

Amelia opened her mouth and Louisa smiled, feeling for the first time that she'd made a right decision.

"In the future, you can arrange his clothes, but this time, while you're re-establishing your funds, allow me. "

CHAPTER

EIGHT

Albert didn't sleep a wink. As the hours ticked by, he paced and watched, read, and picked up a pen to write in his journal, but the words didn't come. How could they? In the morning old Mr Brumfells from Brumfells, Anstead, and Hills Solicitors would arrive and bring with him the last will and testament of his father, his brother having passed only three weeks prior to his father's death.

Now seated in the dining room, he picked at the breakfast he'd been offered. The only thing that sat somewhat comfortably in his stomach was the tea... weak and cool.

The door opened and Frederick wandered in, his dark, wavy hair a foil to his camel-coloured pants and plain, white shirt. His waistcoat, of dark green, unbuttoned and flapping as he moved. "You didn't sleep well."

Albert shrugged. "Too much on my mind. Today, my life officially changes, and I learn what damage was done. What needs to be rectified, and any other aspects of my life which will be forever changed." The words erupted in a snarl, and he sighed, closing his eyes. "I'm sorry, Fred. I just..." What more was there to say?

Fredrick shut the dining room door, and Albert lifted the cup to his mouth and sipped, but now it was stewed—cold and bitter, and he set the cup aside.

"What time do you expect—?"

A loud knock sounded through the house, and Albert's stomach lurched.

He rose and strode to the door, opening it wide. He needed to know the moment it began. The new life.

His man opened the front door, and while the footman and gentleman couldn't see him, Albert noted as an older, stooped gentleman gave his card.

"Yes, Mr. Brumfells, the master is awaiting you." The footman ushered him inside the house.

Sucking in a deep breath, he waited until the man was escorted to the door of the room, which was open. Albert had a brief second of hesitation, should he sit or move away? But that passed and the knock came at the door. "Mr Brumfells, sirs."

"Come in," he answered and watched as the man made his way forward.

"Your Grace, I'm Roland Brumfells, from Brumfells, Anstead, and Hills in London. I have the last will and testament of your father. Are you ready?" He eyed Frederick, and Albert had no illusions that the man wished his friend gone.

"Please take a seat, Mr Brumfells." He turned to the footman. "Coffee, then leave us until I ring." The footman nodded and withdrew. Another servant, a young maid, scurried into the room to clear the table as Frederick made to rise. "No, stay, Fred. I'd welcome your thoughts."

Brumfells tugged off his glasses with a frown. "Sir, I'm not sure... Usually, we talk only with the recipients..."

"No, I believe Frederick would be wise remaining. Another person to hear and pick apart if you will." He took his place at the head of the table, settling into the padded seat and waiting.

Quickly, the coffee service was brought in, the housemaid pouring cups then withdrawing and leaving them to their business.

Brumfells opened his leather satchel and withdrew a large, folded parchment wad. "Very well then. Let me begin."

He read through the text; it was dry and heavily imbued with *wherewithal* and *thereafter's*. At the end, Albert's head spun.

"So let me get this right. My father left anything that was entailed to me."

"Indeed, Your Grace. However, the bulk of the gifts, shall we say, were to a Jane Finemore. However, we've made a range of efforts to track the lady down and been quite unsuccessful. Our man is seeking her, however, given the estate was meant for your brother, who predeceased the Earl by three weeks and two days, most unfortunate that was, then that puts the entire estate in jeopardy. We will need to make application to the Probate Court as to how we should apportion—"

"But as I am the ninth Earl of Conney, does that not override the terms of the portioning of the estate?" Albert wondered aloud.

"On the tied estate, yes. However, since we are unable to find Miss Finemore, and almost a year has passed since the previous Earl died…" He spread his hands. "We have intelligence that says she may be deceased, however, we are looking for evidence of the same. Not that there is much to grant. A painting, some letters and items that hold little financial value."

"Who was she?" Frederick enquired.

Brumfells blushed. "We believe she was a paramour of his from his earlier days. Before he met the countess. He kept her in accommodation and paid her bills."

"Ahh," Albert intoned. "His mistress."

"Indeed. Now sir, we will make application for the probate based on the information at hand. We've already managed to complete the majority of the documentation required, but signatures will be needed. And witnesses." He shuffled through the papers, his white hair falling over his eyes. "Ah, yes." He tugged out a pen. "Once this is completed, I'll be able to give you the letters meant for you and your brother. I also have your mother's final will and testament. She gave specific instructions it was only to be dealt with on your return, and I'll be pleased to hand you the keys to her property. She also had a healthy account, and I'm sure your man of business—"

"Corvings..."

"Ah yes, Emile Corvings. He will have briefed you somewhat. There is a secondary bequest, and a small package for you. We'll get to that in a moment. Now, if you could sign here." He slid the paper and a large pen toward Albert.

He didn't scan the page to find what it read, simply affixed his signature as indicated, 'there, there, and there.'

"My mother's will?"

"Indeed, she left the bulk of her estate to you. It is a reasonable-sized holding. However, with the death of your brother, all his effects will also be conferred on you as he was intestate. Probate will begin in the matter of his estate, though largely it is merely his clothing as everything else was cleared to finalise his not insubstantial debts. The monetary bequest she made to him was already used. There was a smaller packet for him, however, that was not to be made available to him until his marriage. As that never took place, you also receive that. She was very clear that you were to come into your inheritance, unlike your brother, immediately."

All very strange. Why have two different situations for us? But then he considered that even as a younger man, his brother had been a wastrel. Money and items had little value to him, and perhaps, whatever it was that he should have inherited had monetary value and she feared he would pawn it and use the proceeds in a gaming hell?

Another wad of papers, more signatures.

Mr Brumfells removed two small, brown paper wrapped packages from his bag and slid them across the table. "Do you wish me to wait...?"

"No. I'll call on you in London soon to finalise my will."

"Any specific bequests?" Brumfells enquired.

"Yes, my home and property in the colony is to be bequeathed to Frederick Hollis. My mother's estate as well in the event I do not marry and have children. The estate, will of course, go with the title."

He caught sight of Frederick who sat there open-mouthed. "You... You can't!"

Albert shrugged. "Only if I don't marry and have children. I've years ahead of me, as have you."

Brumfells cleared his throat. "That is most irregular."

"Perhaps, but that's my will. Draw it up, and when I'm in London, I'll sign it in your office."

As far as dismissals went, it was clear, and the man rose, nodded, and took his leave. Albert glanced down at the packages.

"Open them, Albert," urged his friend.

He both wanted to and didn't want to. On one hand, he knew this would be the last thing he received from his mother, but also what could they be?

The first item came undone as he tugged on the string and out tumbled a strand of pearls, two rings, and he noted the wrapping was a letter.

Thomas,

The strand of pearls was given to me by my parents on my wedding day. As my first born, it is right that they are passed to you, however, I would implore you to gift them to your bride.

The rings were my mother and grandmother's, given to them on their come out. Each has been held by me since their passing. They should be passed to your daughters or children as they have been kept within the family and worn for over one hundred years. Treasure them, for these are a connection to those long gone.

I wish you a happy life with your new bride and hope that she might help you to find peace in yourself, the peace that you never found during my lifetime.

Your mother,

Constance Cimmaron

The writing was spidery, the letters fading on the hazed parchment, but he couldn't help himself tracing her name at the bottom of the missive. It was so like her to wish Thomas well even though he'd treated her abominably.

The second package was larger, misshapen. His hand shook as he reached for and tugged on the string.

Out tumbled two jewellers' boxes, a journal, and a faded photo. Of him and her. Tears burned his eyes.

He opened the first leather-bound box, and a small ruby and pearl ring lay nestled next to a plain gold band. He knew them well, as she'd worn them every day of her life. The second contained a necklace and earring set. Old-fashioned and heavy but with a quiet beauty set in dull gold. The pale stones he thought might have been sapphires or similar. Inside that box was also a brooch. The same pale stones with a dull gold setting, and a final ring. Small and set with a similar stone. He didn't know these pieces but felt sure they were special.

He turned to the letter. The journal he wouldn't open yet.

Dearest Albert,

How I wish you were here and I could hand these pieces to you. I sent both yours and your brother's inheritance to the solicitors once I realised I might not recover from this illness. It was vitally important to me that you receive them.

My father's estate will be yours. That was agreed on your birth, and I ensured your father had that agreement in writing. I loved your father once, but after Thomas' birth he changed. By the time you were born, he was cold and only interested in himself and Thomas. I wish he'd never sent you away, but he was too strong, and I wasn't able to stop him. I wished, every day, for your return. You were always a quiet and thoughtful child. The one I could count on to stand up for those weaker. In the case of Frederick Hollis, I did write to those I knew, those connections I'd made in society, but as a woman I was unable to overcome the indenture. I know, one day, you will make right what your father did. What Thomas did was wrong, for Thomas was the one who stole the watch. But he was your father's heir, and no one would believe when I said he was the culprit.

I have made arrangements for Frederick's family. It's not a lot, but they will be cared for. I had them sent to my father's estate. I never told anyone else and bade they not share that information either. Forgive me for not waiting for your return, but I hope in some small way, you will understand the importance of the items I sent you.

The matching set were my grandmothers. She wore them on her wedding day, as did my mother and I. They were never part of my dowry and were returned to her for safekeeping. I pray one day you find a woman you will give them to. That she may wear them for her wedding. That you will be happy.

I have ever loved you, son.

Your mother,

Constance Cimmaron

CHAPTER
NINE

Albert waited in silence within the foyer of the grand home. This was to be his first foray back into society and he felt at sea. Where his brother would have come and gone, he felt lost.

"What am I doing here?" he muttered and slid a shaking finger under the band constricting his neck.

"We could leave," murmured Frederick.

He nearly accepted the suggestion. Indeed, he turned to answer. But then his gaze strayed to the door and his heart ceased beating the refrain it had kept for over thirty years.

That's when he saw her, the woman of beauty. The woman he'd spied at the hotel. Tonight, she wore a midnight blue gown, which lovingly traced her tall, lush form. Her hair, piled high, shone in the light of the chandelier, and he almost swallowed his tongue. Beside her was another woman, not a raving beauty but with a quiet inner glow in a lavender gown, her light brown hair pulled back into a less formal knot. She worried her gloves, if the bobbing of her fan were an indication.

His gaze returned to the beauty. She smiled and turned to the couples behind her, answered some question, then the crowd shifted.

"We need to move forward, Albert," Frederick spoke, breaking the magical spell.

But he felt her presence, the air tingling.

They shuffled forward and finally were admitted.

A servant stopped them at the doorway. "Your name, sir?"

"The Earl of Conney, and Mr Frederick Hollis."

The man bowed deeply, and Albert heard the waves of whispers. "Conney," and "The missing Earl," were muttered.

His name was broadcast to the room, and he entered, aware that eyes were turned in his direction.

They made their way down the stairs and into the middle of the guests. "Your Grace." An older woman he presumed to be the hostess reached out her hand. "It is our great pleasure to have your attendance this evening. Allow me to introduce my husband, the Duke of St Croix."

He bowed to the man in his middle years and was relieved that it was returned.

Not a word was spoken by the man, but there was a smile on his face, and Albert breathed a little easier as he moved down the receiving line, meeting the son and daughter of the Duke and Duchess.

Once he'd processed to the end he stopped and turned.

"Mrs Louisa Lavenwood, and Mrs Amelia Cartwright."

His vision in blue flowed down the steps, into the middle of the ball, appearing comfortable in the surroundings, followed by the Viscount and Viscountess of Traughton and Lord and Lady Ravenhelm.

The moment unfolded. Louisa's name was called, and she slid forward, Amelia at her side. "Smile, Amelia. We are the centre of attention, and we will enjoy it."

"I'd rather give birth again," muttered her new friend, and it took every ounce of discipline to stop herself from laughing at the comment.

The one thing she'd learned with certainty about Amelia was that when the situation was all-consuming, her friend would throw out some line that made her smile because they were usually aimed at taking the sting from the current situation or gauged to remove the gravity.

"Mrs Lavenwood, it is so good to make your acquaintance finally. Why, it's a night for social highs as the new Earl of Conney has also entered society. Now, allow me to introduce my husband, the Duke of St Croix."

Louisa dropped into a low curtsey and noted Amelia did the same. She almost hid her smile at the smoothness of the other woman's action. They'd both been well-schooled in such niceties it seemed, though their backgrounds might be dissimilar.

"And this is my son, Franklin, and daughter Emily." Polite pleasantries were exchanged, and Louisa turned, but before she could melt into the crowd, the Duchess took her hand. "Allow me to introduce the Earl of Conney, and his friend, Mr Frederick Hollis."

She turned and the breath in her lungs fled. Before her was a handsome stranger. His light reddish blond hair closely cropped, piercing blue eyes, and perfect oval visage was before her. "A pleasure, Mrs Lavenwood. Mrs Cartwright. My friend, Frederick Hollis."

It took a moment for her to properly regain her wits. "The pleasure is all mine, sir. Mr Hollis."

The Earl took her hand, and the frisson of awareness sparked through her.

"Louisa, dear, do introduce us," Elspeth called behind her, and Louisa jumped.

"Of course, this is the Earl of Conney, and Mr Hollis." Her voice came out different somehow, deeper and throatier than before.

She turned to Amelia and was surprised to find her friend looking at Mr Hollis, her mouth slightly open and eyes dilated.

"It's my pleasure, sir," Conney said, taking Aeddan's hand. The interplay of introductions took place around her, and suddenly, once again, there was silence.

"Would you..." Conney cleared his throat. "Would you care to take a turn around the room with me? I know no one here."

She smiled, feeling a little more balanced. "I wish I could, but I am entering society for the first time. This... I don't know anyone either, but perhaps, instead of taking a turn, you might wish to join our party for a while?"

She might feel the sudden interest in the man, but Amelia was clearly overwhelmed or smitten or... well, whatever, with the man Hollis. If there was a firm interest, she'd do all she could to give her new friend the opportunity to pursue happiness, she thought with a sudden ferocity.

Indeed, what a smashing idea," Isabelle crowed. "Come, tell us about yourselves, gentlemen." And suddenly the world felt right.

Albert's brain spun. He'd asked Mrs Lavenwood to take a turn and somehow was scooped up into a social situation that eased his and Frederick's entrée into society. Mrs Lavenwood was the centre, and he quickly learned, while new to society, her attendance had been keenly anticipated.

"We have both returned to England from Australia." And before he could say any more the viscountess, who insisted he should call her Elspeth, was peppering him with questions about the strange fauna. She'd heard of the koala and kangaroo, and had also heard stories of creatures that swam in waters yet were deadly.

"The platypus," he explained "lays eggs and is quite dangerous if one ignores the spines on their legs, while strangely beautiful. I've only ever seen one once. Frederick and I don't live in an area where it rains much, as we herd sheep, but yes, when we took up our properties, we travelled where they were."

"Fascinating," Isabelle answered with a smile.

Of course, while he participated in the social chatter, he was aware he needed to raise Frederick's cause. But this wasn't the time. No, instead he'd arrange to meet with the viscount at a later point to seek his assistance in clearing Fred's name.

Right now, he basked in the nearness to the woman he now knew as Mrs Lavenwood. *Louisa.* He wondered if she knew he was her neighbour, but it was another fact he'd keep to himself, and perhaps he'd take it upon himself to call on her tomorrow.

Others floated into the social circle, introductions were made, and when he thought it was time to withdraw from their circle, the viscount himself asked him to stay as he enquired about the land, the arable farming areas, and the wider plains suitable for cattle grazing and sheep.

Frederick too participated in the conversations, but it was the woman, Mrs Lavenwood, who captured Albert's attention.

"I believe the land is much hotter than here. My sisters have travelled to India and China and have told me of strange animals and steamy summer weather," Mrs Lavenwood said.

"It can be, once you traverse the blue mountains."

"Blue? Are they really?"

He couldn't help the smile. "From a distance, they can appear so. They have been a barrier for a long time to travellers, but the land beyond is excellent for certain grazing and agricultural practices."

"Indeed. That would be most interesting to see."

A footman slid up to her and handed a note. She paled, but didn't open it.

"Is all well?" Albert enquired.

She smiled and answered, "All is fine." But it clearly wasn't as her pupils dilated and the beautiful, creamy skin of her face had paled.

Her hands scrunched up the missive, and he didn't miss the white-knuckle grip she kept on it.

"If you'll excuse me, I need a moment." With that she whirled away and left him.

It was all very strange, but he was a new-comer and what could he do?

&

It took every ounce of willpower for Louisa to withdraw into a quiet corner, but her gaze darted here and there. She'd be damned if the woman was going to corner her though.

Several deep breaths helped to clear the fog that threatened to envelop her brain. Damn it, she'd finally made it this far. How could that damned—

With her mind racing, she indicated to a nearby manservant.

"Yes, madam?"

"Could you please arrange for the Lavenwood carriage? I feel a little unwell and will leave."

The man bowed deeply, and she had a thought he'd probably dealt with something similar before. A hysterical laugh bubbled up, but she ruthlessly pushed it down. Not here and not now.

She spied the group, Amelia standing to the side with the Earl of Conney who looked desperately out of place, as did his friend, Mr Hollis. The Earl had been interesting and not at all the vapid banter she'd expected. An adventurer and a landowner.

Tears stung as she made her way out of the shadowy corner and headed for Amelia. Much as she might like to let her stay, it would be unseemly. "Amelia?"

The woman raised her head. "You're unwell?"

She reached a trembling hand to her friend. How had she understood with only days of knowing each other? "I think we should leave," she murmured, and Amelia nodded.

Louisa captured her sister Elspeth's gaze, staring into her eyes.

Elspeth nodded though Louisa refused to tell her sister everything. After all, that would only make things worse here. She'd find Pamela Jezerey and give her a piece of her mind, in front of everyone. Scandal was one thing Louisa hoped to avoid. And the missive still balled in her hand felt like a beacon, one she didn't want her sister to know about.

"Mrs Lavenwood, is all well?" the Earl once again questioned, and she smiled.

"I am feeling a trifle under the weather and will take my leave." Then she pulled away, but something about the man had her glancing back, only to see him watching her as she withdrew.

Once safely in the carriage, Amelia cleared her throat. "Whatever that is in your hand, you're holding it very tightly."

Louisa sighed. "It's a letter. From Lady Pamela Jezerey."

Amelia looked at her, and Louisa understood she didn't know who Louisa was talking about. "The woman Jeremy had a child with before he died. The one who thinks..."

"She wrote to you? At a ball?"

"I don't think she wrote this today, but was hopeful she'd find me. She's not welcome in most houses and would only be at the larger balls. The ones that are more open to individuals."

Amelia frowned. "But a Duke and Duchess..."

"I don't know how all this works in detail, but Elspeth says that in Brighton, one can be a little less strict with invitations. That the balls are bigger, for they are less stringent in the choice of who attends. It makes the location an excellent testing ground for someone like me."

"What's wrong with you, Louisa? You're well-born and comfortable. You are a widow and entering society..."

Amelia's heartfelt support buoyed Louisa, but the truth was, entering London society would be harder. She'd need to be ready for the ordeal. A house of an acceptable size, her wardrobe of the highest calibre, and her sisters would need to support her in order to find entrée. It was easier than it had been, with the number of American heiresses marrying into the highest houses, but there were still restrictions and requirements she'd have to meet.

"It's not as simple as that, Amelia. In London even the whisper of Lady Pamela and my husband and her wanting—"

"Wanting what?" Amelia pounced on the poor word choice.

Louisa closed her eyes, counted to five, then reopened them. "She wants money to go away. She has a child to raise, and her husband refuses to do so."

"But that was your husband."

"Yes. But that's the problem, he was my husband. What was the reason he strayed? Why did he choose her instead of me? He had another child." Tears threatened, and this time she didn't care. They dripped down her cheeks as she looked away. "I didn't give him a son, I only had daughters. He was running through my dowry, and if it hadn't been for Corvings, I'd be left near destitute. I loved him. He didn't love me, not really. So, now I pay the price."

Amelia reached out and took her hand. "Society is most unfair. But he's gone now and—"

"She sent me this." Louisa thrust the missive into Amelia's hands, sure that the other woman would understand.

I see you.
You think I don't know you? That I won't tell the world how your husband strayed and foisted his child on another man? How I had a child that you ignored? That you failed in every way that a woman should be able to fulfill her husband.
It will all be revealed.
Of course, if you wish to keep the secret, you could direct your man of business to simply make the payment. I'll be watching.
P

"That... That witch!" Amelia raised her eyes. "But can't you—"

"What? Oust her? Publicly humiliate her? That's what she's threatening to do to me. I won't stoop to her level." Her voice sounded tight, but she was holding it all in, trying to contain the fury, frustration, and hurt.

"I wish I could help you. You're doing so much for me and—"

"I like your company. You're soothing and have a solid head on your shoulders. You're easy to have around, and your little boy is a treasure. The girls already adore him. He's like the brother they don't have."

"Louisa?" Amelia spoke softly, as if to soothe Louisa's emotional distress.

"Except they have another sibling." She dashed at the tears as the house came into view.

The carriage rolled to a stop, and as soon as the door was open, she was out and to the door.

"It's not your fault, Louisa. You didn't make the decisions," Amelia called from behind her.

No, she hadn't. But she'd been unaware of what was happening, living in the little bubble of self-assurance. Hiding from the truth.

Albert reined in his mount, the town still asleep for the most part, and he enjoyed the freedom. Frederick had remained at the house this morning, but Albert needed to clear his mind. The ball must have continued well into the wee hours, but he'd left around midnight, his body urging him to find rest. "Too many years of early mornings."

Before him, another rider came into view, moving slowly, and he waited until they rode closer.

A woman... Louisa Lavenwood.

She glanced up, her veil concealing her face until she drew nearer. It was pale and drawn, with deep circles ringing her eyes.

"Mrs Lavenwood." He touched his hand to the brim of his hat.

"Your Grace."

They drew up next to each other, her mount a muscular chestnut. "A beautiful horse."

She smiled. "Lightning was a gift from my sisters."

"I must make do with a rented nag."

"Perhaps, but he's lovely." She reached out and ran her hand over the neck of his horse.

"You like horses?"

"I like to ride. It's... I can be alone for a short while when I ride out." Louisa shook her head. "Elspeth and Isabelle would have hysterics if they knew, but I need the air. I need to think and sometimes this is the only way."

He cocked his head. "You have something that is causing you distress, and this is your time to consider it?"

Her expression changed, became guarded. "I'm not sure..."

I need to change the conversation. He didn't quite understand why not losing her regard ranked so highly, but it was important to him. "Mrs Lavenwood, may I call on you later today?"

She opened her mouth and closed it again. Blinked once then again. "I... Of course." The words were slow, and he realised that she was taken by surprise. "I will be at home today."

"Excellent. Now, if you're amenable, I would be happy to escort you home."

She opened her mouth again, then closed it as a carriage rumbled past. "Yes. Thank you."

He wheeled his horse, feeling a little more comfortable than he had when he'd left the house, and he refused to examine why. It didn't matter; he'd achieved exactly what he'd hoped. They rode in companionable silence until they neared the houses. "Until later, Mrs Lavenwood."

He waited for the stable hand to take control of her reins and ensured she had dismounted before riding on to the stables a street away. Once the horse was safely handed over, he made his way back to the house, whistling as he walked.

The house loomed when a sound echoed behind him, and he

whirled in time to catch sight of a fist. Albert dodged and flicked out a leg, tripping his attacker.

"What do you want?" No time for niceties, thugs didn't attack without something in mind. Something they wanted.

The man lurched up, barrelling into him, but Albert took the split second to prepare himself for the move.

The man's eyes boggled. He reared back as if aware that he was about to tussle with a man who knew how to fight and wasn't sure about his opponent. "Aint worth the money," he growled, turned, and fled.

Albert didn't chase him, as the other man was fast, and he didn't need the inconvenience at this point.

CHAPTER

TEN

Louisa settled herself on the chair and waited, well aware that she would have callers this morning. Elspeth had sent her a missive, asking if she'd like her in attendance, as had Isabelle. Louisa had replied that today she should be fine for the morning and that her sisters should take their time. That she'd see them later in the day as they prepared for the opera they were to attend this evening.

Amelia settled into the chair nearby, sipping on a cup of tea. "You look more rested, Louisa."

Her fingers twined. "I rode this morning."

"I haven't ridden in such a long time," Amelia murmured.

"Why?"

"Because I didn't have time to ride. My husband worked out of the house, and I had a child at home. There wasn't time or money for a horse either."

"We could... Let's plan a riding party then. Something where you can—"

"But I don't have..." Amelia cleared her throat. "...clothing or horse, and I'm not sure how long I could ride for either."

Louisa smiled. "Those are easy problems to overcome. We can arrange a habit for you, and as to a horse, I can purchase one. Something quiet I suspect is what you'd be best mounted on. Besides, the girls and your son will need lessons soon. So, it seems appropriate to purchase a mount suitable for their lessons too."

Amelia opened her mouth, and Louisa raised her hand. "As for practice, I ride most mornings, so it's no hardship. We can both ride in the morning if that suits you?"

Amelia nodded.

The sound of a knock echoed, and Louisa sat up a little straighter in her seat, waiting for the servant to bring them in, should they be guests Louisa and Amelia should meet with.

The door was opened by Millie, who bobbed a curtsey before stepping aside. The Earl of Conney and his friend Mr Hollis stepped into the room. Amelia smiled shyly at Mr Hollis, while Conney made his thanks to Louisa for allowing him to call, then settled on the chair nearest her.

Warmth filled Louisa as he engaged her in conversation. "I enjoyed our meeting earlier today."

"As did I," returned Louisa. "Amelia and I were just saying we should plan a riding party. There are many pretty landmarks we may visit nearby. We could ride out, take a picnic, and make a day of it."

"That's an excellent idea. I'm sure both Fred and I would be happy to attend should we be included."

"Then we shall put our heads together and plan something soon. Will you be attending the opera tonight?"

The Earl nodded. "Yes. We were invited by the viscount last night."

Louisa grinned. Something about that made her feel warm deep inside, and she couldn't contain the burst of pleasure. She glanced to Amelia and noted the light blush on her cheeks, as she sat together with Mr Hollis on the other side of the room.

"Your friend is paying attention to Amelia. It's very kind as she's quite uncomfortable in social settings."

The Earl frowned. "Yes, Frederick hasn't had an easy life, and he's a good friend. But she should be aware that his property is in Australia. Should there be any interest—"

Louisa heard the concern. "I'm not sure Amelia has plans on his offering her marriage."

"Perhaps," the Earl answered. "Now, tell me, you have daughters?"

"Yes, two, Eleanora and Marina. Eleanora is four, and Marina two."

"I don't have children or nieces and nephews, but I have an overseer with children. They're boisterous but happy."

Her smile slipped a little. "Eleanora has been ill recently, but is recovering. It's been a period of upheaval for them. We moved from home to here, and many of the people they know were left behind."

"You're making a lot of changes, when most would be comfortable to stay where they are."

She bit her lip. "It was the best time. I'll be looking for a governess for Eleanora soon, and I feel that now, with the changes in my life, this was the right choice. It has been a wrench, but they are settled so long as Nanny and I are with them."

He shifted in the chair, and she wasn't sure what more he wanted to know.

"Would you like a cup of tea?"

"That would be delightful. I'm sure Fred would welcome it too," the Earl answered.

She turned and rang the bell, seeking a moment to find her centre again. When Millie entered, she smiled. "Fresh tea and cups. Thank you, Millie."

The girl bobbed and withdrew.

Frederick turned. "I was in Ceylon for some time and saw how they make tea."

Louisa turned. "Really? I would think it's quite time-consuming."

"It certainly takes a lot of men to grow, harvest and produce a quality tea. It was interesting, but I was much happier once I arrived in Australia. It's not tea-growing area, but there's a beauty other countries cannot capture."

"You've travelled a lot, Mr Hollis," Amelia offered.

"I was... It was a personally difficult time, but I must also say I'm grateful I had the opportunities to travel and see parts of the world that others will not. It gave me a wider appreciation of what I have."

Every conversation Albert had with Louisa Lavenwood told him she was a woman who was looking to find her way in a man's world. One who was willing to help others while entering society. She was warm and giving. All he had to do was look at how she included her friend that he now understood was a paid companion.

The woman Frederick was showing definite interest in.

Louisa was the kind of woman Albert would be more than happy to have as a wife. They could converse without the vacuousness of insipid misses. She'd lived and loved and lost. She was used to responsibility. If he was merely the Earl, she'd be perfect.

He sat in the parlour, nursing his whiskey while waiting for Frederick to join him before the opera.

If all he had to worry about was finding a life partner, it would be simple. She'd be the kind of woman he'd pursue. But it wasn't that simple. He had the added responsibilities of the estate and his mother's manor.

And this morning's assailant... That also sat uncomfortably, because there had to be more to it. It wasn't the kind of thing that came out of nowhere.

On a whim, he rose and settled at the desk in the corner. Tugged out a sheet of paper and took up the pen.

Corvings,
Could you please confirm the whereabouts of Storck? I had a rather

surprising and unwelcome visit this morning and am suspicious
that he was behind the visitation.
Yours,
Albert Montclair

He folded the paper and slid it into an envelope he tugged from the drawer and wrote *Corvings* on the outside. "Sproggs?"

The man popped his head around the door. "Sir?"

"Will you arrange to direct this to my man, Corvings? I believe he's in residence at the Great Brighton Hotel. If not, he's likely returned to his office in London." He handed over the envelope.

"Indeed. First thing in the morning, sir. Now will you be requiring...?"

"Only my carriage. Oh, and send around to the livery again. I'll ride out in the morning," Albert replied. Frederick entered the room, tugging on the collar of his jacket. "You'll ride with me in the morning?"

"Uh, yes. I will, thank you, Albert."

"Very good, sirs. I will make the arrangements immediately." Sproggs then withdrew, and Albert took the final swallow of his drink.

"Then we should be away." Albert rose and headed for the door. "Mrs Cartwright and Mrs Lavenwood are both set to attend tonight."

Frederick's eyes gleamed. "I shall enjoy their company. Very much."

Or at least Mrs Cartwright's.

CHAPTER
ELEVEN

The carriage pulled up at the building, the theatre Royal Brighton, which at first glance Louisa thought to be old, maybe not quite a century, but still. Lights gleamed in the sconces though, and it appeared both well cared for and popular, if the number of carriages drawing up were anything to judge by.

The door opened, and she was assisted from the carriage, followed by Amelia. Together they made their way inside the foyer, and Aeddan and Elspeth, together with Isabelle and Langdon, waited.

Their cloaks were removed and taken for storage as glasses of champagne were pressed into their hands. "It's quite popular tonight." Louisa scanned the room.

"Indeed. The performance tonight should be enjoyable. It's Mr Gilbert and Mr Sullivan's *Pirates of Penzance*. I've seen it once, and it's exceptionally clever," Isabelle offered.

"I have heard of it," added Amelia. "It's meant to be funny, I believe?"

Just as Elspeth was about to answer the query, judging by the way she opened her mouth, a commotion sounded at the door and

Louisa turned to watch the Earl of Conney enter. He was truly a magnificent man, if only she were looking for another husband, she reminded herself.

"Ah, here comes the rest of the party. Mr Hollis and Your Grace, it's a pleasure to see you once again." Langdon smiled as he welcomed the men.

Drinks were proffered and they made small talk until it was time to move to the booth her brother-in-law had obtained for the evening.

They settled into their seats, ladies taking the front row and the gentlemen behind them. Louisa was supremely aware that the Earl was sitting just behind her, and she imagined the whisper of his breath at the nape of her neck. It was *disconcerting* to say the least. Her body was reacting in ways it never had before, and the sensations left her... *tingling*!

"Have you seen this before?" the Earl queried her quietly, and Louisa turned.

"No. I hadn't heard of it before."

"I've heard tell, but rarely do I have the chance to see such performances," he elaborated.

"No. I would think you'd be busy for most of the hours of the day. I mean, with cattle and..." She wracked her brain, attempting to remember what animals he ran.

"Sheep," he corrected as if reading the scrambled mess in her mind. "I only have sheep."

"Yes, sheep."

"It's more about the time away from my property," he added.

"But surely someone must be attending to it while you are here? I mean, they'd need to be sheared and..."

Louisa wanted to curse herself for the shallowness of her comments, but he smiled. "I have an overseer I trust. He's taking care of business at my property and assisting with Fred... Mr Hollis' too."

"You seem to be good friends. You've known him a long time?"

"We grew up together, until circumstances sent us off on

different paths. Purely by accident we met again, and he worked with me for some time until he was able to take a selection of his own, his boundary adjoins my property." He frowned, and Louisa wondered why he appeared so ill at ease when speaking about this friend.

"You seem a bit... concerned?" she queried, and his brows pulled together.

"I... I need to discuss his situation with the viscount. Not tonight but soon. He has connections and Frederick was... He was blamed for something he didn't do. Not transported but sent away as an indentured servant."

Now it was Louisa's turn to feel surprise. "I... That's awful. I mean, I didn't think that kind of thing could happen in a civilised society."

He grimaced. "My father was involved, as was my brother. I need to have Frederick's name cleared."

She bit her lip. "Would you like me to raise it with Aeddan?"

"No," he spoke hurriedly. "I appreciate that, but it's difficult and I'd rather undertake it."

She waited, hoping he'd elaborate further.

"I feel responsible. It was my family, and it sits poorly." He shifted in his seat. "It appears the piece is about to begin," he said, and she had to turn around. Feign an interest in what was no doubt a very clever rendition, but her mind was caught up, wondering as to the reasons that Mr Hollis should be sent away. What had he done, seen, and experienced?

When the intermission came, she joined the rest of the audience, smiling and clapping. "You've been distracted," Amelia whispered as they left the box and joined the others milling in the private area.

"I apologise. We can discuss it later though," she answered and saw a gleam of interest in Amelia's gaze.

"Indeed. You seemed in deep conversation with the Earl before the play began," Isabelle said, with a sly smile on her face.

"Don't try and matchmake, sister. I'm too old, and a widow besides," Louisa said with a bite in her voice and her body tensing.

Isabelle's smile melted, and Louisa immediately felt a pang seeing her sister's reaction.

"I'm sorry. I should control my tongue. Jeremy always said..." Louisa stopped herself. It was the first time she'd raised his name in this kind of conversation and she wondered at it. She'd felt horrendously hurt and betrayed by his actions, but now, she wondered if his actions were more because he didn't truly love her. Oh, he'd said he had, and his family had made the push for him to offer. She'd known that and been only too eager to accept. Maybe... Maybe they'd both made mistakes and she needed to let go of her frustration at him? Maybe that was the path to starting a new life?

"Jeremy was a perfect beast to you," Isabelle muttered.

"I think we both were not good for each other. In hindsight, I should have seen the signs and known better. I was young and headstrong, Isabelle." She reached out and touched her sister's hand. "I need to let go of my anger. I need to be happy again."

"That doesn't mean you can't marry."

She cocked her head. "I don't need a husband to be happy."

"But it does make life easier," Amelia offered with a shy smile.

"Would you marry again?" Elspeth asked.

"Perhaps. For the right reasons." Amelia's answer left Louisa confused, so it was just as well the men re-joined them at that moment.

Albert jumped out of bed, and it took a moment to understand why he was so enthused, then he remembered. He and Frederick were riding today. They'd be joined by the ladies from next door.

He dressed quickly, but with care, ensuring his coat was neat and wrinkle-free.

Mrs Lavenwood was witty and lovely.

Mrs Lavenwood had also featured in his dreams and his body had reacted as anticipated. Unfortunately, it wasn't really something he'd planned or even necessarily wanted. Oh, if she'd been the kind of woman who enjoyed a liaison, perhaps he'd be tempted, but she didn't strike him as that kind of woman. No, she clearly deserved happiness and forever, if the little he'd overheard in the lounge last night was to be believed.

He was ready and downstairs waiting when Frederick emerged, smiling.

"You look very pleased with yourself," Albert observed.

"I am," Frederick replied. "Mrs Cartwright is a lovely woman."

Albert blinked. "Indeed. Are you interested?"

Frederick shrugged. "I don't know yet, but I am looking forward to getting to know her. She is sweet and kind and—"

"We'd best not keep the ladies waiting then, had we?"

Once they'd collected their mounts, they made their way to the house next door, and saw the women mounted on their horses. To Albert's eye, the one Mrs Cartwright sat was quiet and steady. Not plump but certainly well-padded. Then his attention turned to Mrs Lavenwood.

"Good morning, sir," she said.

"Mrs Lavenwood." He gave a short nod.

"Louisa," she corrected, and he had to control the surprise and pleasure that stole through him.

"Louisa," he returned, and she smiled. "My name is Albert." His stomach knotted as he waited for her to repeat it.

"Good morning, Albert," she said, and he detected a slight huskiness to her voice. "Amelia hasn't ridden for a long time, and perhaps Mr Hollis would be pleased to keep pace with her?" Her smile reinforced that Mrs Cartwright was perhaps just as interested as Frederick in deepening their acquaintance.

They moved forward, and Albert watched as she raised her head to the air, inhaling deeply.

"I love the scent of the ocean," she said. "I was raised by it and miss it when I'm away."

His stomach contracted at her words. "You don't like to be away from it?"

She turned. "Oh, I don't mind, but it's what I know best. My father was a seaman, he was the founder of Forster Shipping. My sisters and I, we co-own it, but I've not really had much to do with it until now. I'm learning bit by bit, but my sisters are still very much in charge, though I'd dearly like to travel more, like they did."

"They travelled to India and the far east, I believe you said."

"Oh yes, that's where they met their husbands. When they were younger, they travelled with my father too. He encouraged them to become more involved with the family business."

"But not you?" He wanted to know why.

"My aunt stepped in on the death of my mother. Aunt Mary. She said a lady didn't travel like a hoyden, but my sisters were too old to heed her. She passed when I was seventeen, and by then I was too old to really begin, and by my eighteenth birthday I'd married, and it was stay at home and..." Louisa shrugged.

"You wish you'd done more?"

"In hindsight, I was young and self-absorbed. I thought being an adult meant having a household of my own and children. Not that I regret it, for Eleanora and Marina are a joy. I just wish I'd seen things for myself."

They rode on in silence for a while, and he couldn't suppress the feeling that something momentous was happening. They reached the end of the promenade and turned, noting that Mr Hollis and Mrs Cartwright had been left well behind.

"Albert?"

He turned to look at her.

"Why aren't you married?" she asked. He blinked and she coloured up. "Forgive me, that was rude and forward."

"Not at all," he answered. "I've not been in a position until now.

The women I've met, they didn't really seem right, and I guess, the opportunity never rose."

"Has that changed?" Her hand flew up to her mouth, and her eyes grew round. "My mouth is running away this morning."

He smiled, because the surprise and shock on her face was endearing. "I will need to marry, I suppose. As the Earl, it is my responsibility to produce an heir." He hadn't really wanted to consider that side of the situation until now.

She nodded, and by silent agreement, they urged their mounts forward, walking them slowly along the path.

"What about you? You're a widow?"

"Yes. I have two daughters, so that makes it difficult for me. I could marry a man who is older, and who has a family, but most of the eligible men are seeking debutantes. My choices are slim."

The words sat badly, because he could tell she deserved more. She needed someone who would love her, cherish her. Not someone who would use her as a substitute mother for their own children or... Damn it, if only he were able, but he had commitments. The property in Australia.

But the very thought of her with another man set his teeth grinding. It was as if something about her called to him on a deeper level. One he dearly wished he could investigate.

They joined the others in silence, and they rode companionably back to the ladies' house, and when they stopped and bid goodbye, he felt sure some bond between them was stretching the further away he rode.

CHAPTER

TWELVE

Louisa stared at Millie, who was collecting the discarded pot from yet another round of morning 'At Home' calls. "Cook says he lives next door, and that he's got problems on his estate. Something to do with his brother dying and his father spending all the money."

Louisa stood, nerves quivering and jumping in her extremities. Was he simply making an effort with her so he might inveigle her and seize her dowry, like Jeremy had thought to do? Was this about fooling her? She'd made that mistake before, and fear was a thread winding through her mind.

"Thank you," she said, dismissing Millie.

The girl bobbed and took the tea tray, leaving the two women in the room.

Amelia watched as Louisa paced.

"I thought he was different," Louisa muttered.

"Maybe it's not what you think. Perhaps Cook or Millie is wrong?"

Louisa turned. "I made this mistake before," she wailed.

Amelia rose. "I... Mr Hollis said the Earl has invested well. His property in Australia is extensive, and he's working through the situation. I don't know much as Mr Hollis is a loyal friend."

"Do you think...?" Louisa shook her head. "I'm getting ahead of myself though. I mean, he's paying attention, and we ride daily. Perhaps he's just looking for a... for someone to attend society matters with while he's wading through—"

"Mr Hollis said the Earl is trying to clear his name. He's..." Amelia blushed. "Mr Hollis wishes to clear his name now, so he may make future plans."

Louisa stopped, looked at her friend. "Has he made overtures?"

Amelia dropped her head. "No, not really. Nothing definite, but in the weeks we've been acquainted, he's been considerate. He's partnered me at dinners and... Do you think there's a chance?"

Louisa scowled. "It's odd they didn't pay a call this morning." Perhaps Mr Hollis and the Earl had given up on them? She shook her head. "Oh, really. This is silly. After all, the Earl hasn't made any overtures toward me. He's made no promises."

"But you wish he did?" Amelia's words settled at the heart of the matter.

"I... Yes and no. I mean, he's good looking and handsome. Well-connected and well-bred. He has an estate and is..."

"But as a man, Louisa?"

She sighed. Oh yes, nightly her dreams were becoming more heated. Every day she looked forward to his visit, his nearness. "I... As a man, I find him intriguing. I... I like him."

Amelia smiled. "Like? Or more?"

Louisa couldn't help herself as the blush crept up her neck and face, scorching her skin.

"I believe that answers the question then, doesn't it?" Amelia said.

Albert paced the viscount's office.

"You say your father was protecting your brother and trumped up the charge against Mr Hollis here." Aeddan pointed to Frederick where he perched on a chair opposite the heavy desk.

"Yes. He couldn't get anyone to actually say it was Fred, but there were inferences. That's why they didn't try Fred at the assizes or the county court. He said he'd dealt with it personally, as the local magistrate."

Aeddan frowned. "So, you need help to…"

"I need to clear his name," Albert explained.

"And you, Mr Hollis?" Aeddan turned his attention to Frederick.

"I want my name cleared. I've recently come to understand that to achieve the life I want, it's important. Not so much to the person I would like to approach with an offer, but to ensure she and any children we might have aren't burdened. I can live without it, but they shouldn't have to."

Aeddan nodded. "I can make enquiries and work to clear your name, but Albert, your brother's memory—"

He'd thought about this. "He didn't marry or sire any children. My father and mother are gone. Yes, there will be some blowback on me, but Frederick shouldn't have to live with this hanging over his head."

"Fine. I'll make contact with people I know. Since we're talking about futures, Mr Hollis, what is the nature of your interest in Mrs Cartwright?"

Frederick shot a tight smile at the viscount. "Mrs Cartwright is a lovely woman, and I find myself wanting to be with her."

"And your intentions? I ask as head of her family, you understand."

"Honourable, my lord. I will not approach her unless my name is cleared though. I wouldn't do that to her," Frederick answered.

"And her boy?" pressed Aeddan.

"Will be my child too. I wouldn't ask her to abandon him. If I do offer, then it will be with the understanding I want them both. I will cherish them both," Frederick answered, a bite in his voice.

Aeddan smiled. "Then we had best ensure my enquiries are successful." Now he turned to Albert. "And Louisa? You've been paying particular attention. Every day arriving at her gatherings, squiring her at events. Riding with her each morning."

Albert felt the sting of heat on his face. "I am not in a position—"

The frown on Aeddan's face warned him to be careful. "You have no intentions, yet society watches you both. Your actions are building an expectation. If you have no plans, then you need to let her go."

The words punched through Albert. 'Let her go.' If only it were that simple.

He rose. "I'll take your words under advisement." He nodded. "Thank you for your assistance. I will be relocating for the next few days to Conney Hall. Should you have word—"

"I will send a letter. Think over my words, Albert. Louisa has travelled a difficult path and continues to be dogged..." Aeddan sighed. "She's trying hard to stand by herself, and I will not allow anyone to let her fall."

❧

The letter was waiting on Louisa's table when she came downstairs in the morning. There were no identifying marks, simply the words *Mrs Lavenwood* on the outside of the envelope, but the handwriting divulged the name of the sender. "Lady Pamela," she whispered and with shaking hands picked up the packet.

Turning it over, she broke the seal.

Has your gentleman friend learned the truth? That you are unable to keep a man satisfied. Is that why he's left town?

I know who comes and goes and am watching you.
The truth will come out. Unless you agree to my demands.
P

Louisa slumped in the chair. "She's never going to let me go. Not unless I pay her. But I won't." The wobble in her voice betrayed the fears. *Will I ever be free?*

She wiped an unsteady hand over her eyes and turned as the door opened.

The Earl—Albert, her mind corrected—entered the room. "Mrs..." Now she heard his quickened footsteps. "Louisa? What's wrong?"

She hiccupped and clasped a hand over her mouth.

He surged forward and took her hand, the one still holding the missive.

"Please..." she whispered brokenly.

He slid the paper out of her fingers. Raised it. She watched his eyes.

"Who?" he demanded, his lips bracketed with white lines, his face harsh and forbidding.

She shook her head.

"*Who, Louisa?* Who is sending this?" He waved the parchment in the air.

"Je... Jeremy's mistress." The words escaped as a ragged whisper. She couldn't manage more.

"This isn't the first, is it? The wording makes it clear that you know the identity of the author."

"Lady Pamela Jezerey," Amelia answered, entering the room and closing the door. "Forgive me, Louisa. When did that arrive?" She pointed to the letter.

"This morning. It was on the table when I came to sit down."

Albert's hand took hers. "And your brothers-in-law haven't stopped her?"

"I haven't told them, or my sisters, about the letters. It's my problem to solve." She wondered if he'd understand the intent behind the words. After all, he'd not been near in over a week, and she'd keenly felt his absence.

He opened his mouth, then closed it again, and she inwardly groaned. Of course, now that he'd seen that, he'd want nothing to do with her ever again. Any hopes she'd fostered...

"Mrs Cartwright, may I speak with Mrs Lavenwood alone?"

"Of course," Amelia answered, and Louisa saw her friend step away, heard the door open and close.

"Louisa?"

"Why are you here, Albert?" Her chest ached, and she slid her hand free.

"I... I needed to see you. To explain my absence." He shifted from side to side.

"Why?" Louisa croaked.

He shoved his hands into his hair. "I don't..." He shrugged, and she growled.

"Fine!" She stormed across the room, fury replacing the embarrassment and dread. "Please leave."

He turned. "Louisa, I..."

"Go." Her shoulders tensed as she waited.

He advanced and she stepped back, suddenly unsure as a glitter shone in his eyes.

"No, Louisa." He dropped the letter to the floor, reached out and took both her hands in his grip. "No," he repeated, releasing his hands long enough to embrace her.

His arms surrounded her with heat and her breath fled, and when his mouth descended on hers, she... *melted*. His kiss was soft but determined, his hands keeping her where she was.

The kiss lasted forever, or so she thought, and when he released her, she glanced away, touching her lips with shaking fingers.

"Fo... Forgive me." He sounded so stiff, and she looked up to see something close to regret on his face.

"I... There's nothing to forgive." Inside, her heart shattered. "I lost my temper and..."

A grimace came and went. "You did nothing wrong. You asked me to leave and I... I forced you into an embrace. I apologise."

She bit her lip. "I wanted it. Have wanted it." The words slid out.

His eyes widened. "What?"

Louisa shook her head. "Oh dear." She tottered to the lounge and slumped into the seat but not before she noted his advance. "I should learn to keep my mouth shut. Jeremy always..."

"I'm not overly interested in what Jeremy thought or said. You said you wanted it? Did you?" His voice turned silky as he dropped into a crouch before her. "Tell me truthfully, Louisa. Did you want me to kiss you?"

"Yes."

"Damn," he breathed. "I need to think. You need to think, because if I kiss you again, I'm going to want more."

"Oh."

"You know what I mean, Louisa."

"I do."

"Then think. Think hard, and tomorrow, when we ride, we talk. Be ready, Louisa."

Now he rose and left her, wondering what on earth she'd done. What she'd agreed to and what she actually wanted.

Leaving the house was difficult. Albert's body ached with arousal, and his brain told him he should go back in there and demand the satisfaction he was pretty sure she could offer him.

But he wanted more than the coupling. He wanted the connection. He wanted... Damn it, he wanted love. He knew lust was there in spades, but more than that? He just wasn't certain, and with the situation of his home, the mess he'd found in the last week... Unpaid bills, unpaid wages, missing items of value, tenant farmers with lists of demands and property repairs... He wasn't sure he could currently offer any woman the safety of marriage when he didn't know if he could even afford a wife.

The estate was in such a mess.

He also had to marry that up with the situation of Fred. He was still waiting on word from the viscount which was holding his friend back from making an offer of marriage to Mrs Cartwright.

Adding salt to the wound was he'd heard others had begun to take interest in the two women. Men with intent to marry and make them wives.

"I need more time, damn it." He entered the yard and stalked to the front door, which opened before he could knock, and as he stepped in, it was to find chaos.

Two old straw trunks were dumped in the hallway, the door to the parlour ajar and sounds echoing from within.

Taking great care, Albert shed his hat and cane and sidled along the wall, heading toward the door.

He peered inside and stilled. Two women flanked Frederick. Both small and slender, and when they turned, Albert gasped. "Mrs Hollis! Laura!" Fred's mother and sister smiled at him.

"My lord, you brought him back to me! Thank you!" Mrs Hollis limped across the room and enveloped him tightly. "Thank you for caring for my Fred!"

Albert wasn't quite sure how to react, but a warmth flushed him at the happiness he could see on his friend's face, and the way which Fred's sister and mother were reacting. It wasn't why he had made the decisions he'd made, but it was an added benefit he guessed.

Louisa flushed with happiness, the gown she'd been trying on was not quite daring, but certainly displayed her attributes to their best light. She'd moved back into the modiste's parlour and settled beside Amelia when the bell over the door rang.

She didn't pay it much mind, as she considered the material Amelia was holding in her hand while waiting for the young assistant to return with designs Louisa had demanded for Amelia's new wardrobe.

"You really didn't need to buy me more gowns, Louisa," Amelia remonstrated. "I have more than enough."

Louisa clasped her friend's hand. "It's not anything huge, Amelia. I can do this, I've money enough to keep a hundred companions well-dressed and care for their families. And it makes me feel good." She grinned at her friend.

The sound of voices echoed, and Louisa was sure she knew them... She listened intently. Yes! It was... the Earl?

"All bills are to be forwarded to me," he said as two women entered the small withdrawing room before being steered back into a different area. But not before Louisa noted the women. The first one was young and slight. A veritable beauty of svelte figure and light brown hair. Skin like porcelain and eyes of green. The other was an older woman, her features similar to the younger one, but her face was lined and her figure rounded with age.

It was a punch to Louisa's gut, and she gripped her hands into a tight ball, hoping to stave off the cry that rose within her.

"Louisa?" hissed Amelia. "Is it...?"

Louisa stood, moved slightly so she could see through the curtains and noted both men. She nodded to Amelia, well aware her friend was requesting to know if Mr Hollis was also in attendance.

She wanted to scream and cry. Her body felt like ice-water had dashed her, followed by the heat of a flame.

A young seamstress bustled through, but Louisa waylaid her. "Arrange for my carriage to be brought to the back door."

The girl blinked. "Are you unwell…"

"Yes. Now please, hurry." She drew Amelia up and toward the back corner, lest the men see them. She would not suffer the indignity of him knowing she'd seen his paramour, and even worse, that they'd frequented the same establishment.

The young girl returned and bobbed a curtsey. "Your carriage, ladies." She ushered them out the back door, which felt both furtive and private.

Once in the carriage, Louisa tugged the curtains shut, because she had no intentions that he'd see her.

Fury coursed through her veins. Oh yes, another mistake. Another misstep. When would she learn she and men were no good?

Amelia was silent on the ride back to the house, and they entered the front door, sliding off their coats and moving into the parlour.

Louisa watched Amelia sink into the seat that had become her own, hands clasped and face white, while she paced back and forth. "I can't believe I allowed myself…" She sighed. "We've been duped, Amelia."

"I just can't believe what I saw," she whispered.

Neither could Louisa. Her hands shook as she settled at the escritoire, snatched up paper and a pen and began to write.

Dearest Elspeth,
I am ready to look for more than I have. I remember the words you
shared with me after Jeremy passed, about widowhood not being
the end. I want more. Would you meet with me tomorrow morn-
ing? I won't be at home to guests, so we can talk freely.
Louisa

The blunt words felt strange and yet freeing. She'd not really considered the opportunity for a liaison before, but Elspeth and Isabelle had both taken this route. They'd found love—not that she wanted that chain now, but companionship and the intimacy would be welcome.

"What are you doing, Louisa?" Amelia called.

"Something I may, in time, regret, but now?" She shrugged. "I miss having a man at my call. I miss..." She struggled for the words. "I miss being held and touched."

Amelia blushed. "I understand."

"I want something for me. Something where I'm not committed, where it isn't about heirs or love. Something that fulfills me in a way I've never had." Defiance coloured her tone.

"I can't..." Amelia shook her head. "But I will be here and will support you, should you wish to..."

Louisa rose from the seat and walked to Amelia. Crouched before her, and took her hand. "I know. It's both wrong and right."

Albert and Frederick walked up to the door, knocked, and waited to be permitted entry. The butler opened the door, but didn't invite them in. Albert frowned. "Mrs Lavenwood and Mrs Cartwright?"

"They aren't home today, sirs."

She hadn't ridden with them this morning; never mind he'd waited half an hour. There'd been no word, no servant to explain or even a missive. Neither of the ladies had been there. Instead, they'd ridden the horses hard while he worked off his disappointment.

His introspection was broken by the sound of a carriage as it barrelled down the road then came to a stop in front of the house. He watched the carriage door open and both of Louisa's sisters climbed out. He frowned and waited, moving to the side. "Ladies," he said.

They both acknowledged him, and at the door, the butler moved aside to let them pass. Albert waited as the butler bowed low and muttered, "Good day, sirs."

The door shut, and for a long second Albert looked at it then turned to Frederick. "What do you...?"

"I have no idea. Remember, I haven't your position, birth, or experience," Fred muttered.

No, he might not, but something was happening, and she'd shut him out. Figuratively and physically, and he didn't like it. Not one bit.

THIRTEEN

Louisa tugged on the bodice of the gown then frowned. "You're sure?"

Isabelle nodded. "It should be slightly lower, but for a first attempt, it will pass. Now, the object is not to ignore the rules of society, but simply allow them to relax enough that the right men will make themselves known to you."

Louisa had explained her dilemma, though not the underlying reason, to her sisters as they'd gathered in the parlour. Oh, she knew they were just dying to know what had caused this change of heart, but she had no intentions of telling them she was a hair's breadth from devastation.

She'd thought Albert different. She'd have sworn he was special. All she'd got was disappointment. Heat burned in her gut, and she had to push her balled hand against it, hoping it would ease the ache.

Even worse, the latest missive from Pamela had arrived on her doorstep in a basket containing items her husband had clearly left with her prior to his death. A ring Louisa had given him one Christmas, a book of poetry he'd famously read to her before their marriage, and a journal. Each another nail through her heart.

"So, I don't engage in anything other than light flirtation? No arranging assignations and overt displays." Louisa patted her hair. "Amelia, you look lovely in that gown. Elspeth and Isabelle will be with you at any time I'm not, but if you should choose to change your mind—"

"I can't afford to be forward, Louisa. I don't have the connections or money to—"

"I will support you, Amelia. I've already..." But a glance at Amelia's face reinforced that she wouldn't change her perspective. "Fine, then we're ready."

The women pulled on the capes they'd had waiting before they moved to the door. If Louisa had a moment of trepidation about her decision, it was now, as she was leaving her home to enter a new facet of society, one that was unhindered by the same rules.

Climbing into the carriage, she clutched her fingers together tightly, aware once again of the gravitas of her choice. Tonight, she'd set upon looking for a lover. A man who'd fill a need she'd ignored.

At the soiree they climbed from the carriage, and she waited, allowing Amelia to step between her sisters. She'd promised Amelia her reputation would remain untarnished, and if that meant she had to send her ahead, so Louisa entered alone, then so be it.

Divested of her cape, the deep scarlet of her gown twinkled under the thousands of beads which dotted it.

Heads turned, glasses were raised as Louisa straightened up, her serene smile hard won as her name was called and she entered the salon.

Music tinkled and voices swelled as she made her way forward, but only four steps into the room movement heralded to her left and the Earl himself disengaged from the crowds. He stepped before her. "Mrs Lavenwood," he said, and his frown almost warmed the cold centre of her breast. Almost.

"Your Grace. I didn't expect to see you here. I thought you'd be busy. After all, you have guests, I believe." The words slipped loose before she could harness them, and she internally swore. She didn't need him to know, in case he drew the conclusion of jealousy.

"I wasn't aware you knew."

"La! I know many things, sir. But if you'll excuse me?" Louisa stepped to the side, but he kept pace.

"Is something amiss?"

"Not at all." She smiled, hoping it wasn't brittle or telling. "I'm merely here to enjoy myself."

He frowned. "Mrs Cartwright arrived with your sisters."

She watched his face, saw the moment it occurred to him, the way he glanced down to her lower than usual décolletage.

"You can't seriously be thinking... *Louisa*..." He took her arm and marched her to the side of the room, every ounce of her awareness knowing people were talking, whispering.

"You shouldn't manhandle me, Your Grace."

He growled in his throat and tugged her through the door and onto the darkened balcony. Once in a dark corner, he pulled her close. "What game are you playing, Louisa?"

She gulped, because she sensed something dark in him, a rage that wanted to spew forth. "I'm not playing. I just..."

"What? Wanted someone to control that fine body of yours?" he whispered as he pulled her even closer. "Someone to strip you naked and take advantage of your innocence?"

Now she laughed. "Innocence? I've borne two children, I dare say no one would claim me a virgin."

"Virginity be damned, I'm talking about you being a babe-in-arms. You're walking into a den you are unknowing of." His eyes flashed with fire, and God help her, she couldn't stop her mouth.

"The one you know everything about? The women in the modiste's shop appeared so malleable. Which one—"

His mouth crashed down on hers, stopping her words. Savage and darkly desperate as his lips ground over hers.

Her body reacted, firming and melting at the same time. Hunger roaring in her ears, the kind she'd never experienced.

His hand settled on one breast, cupping, and heaven help her, she moaned as he tugged away, and his lips traced a path along her jaw. "Is this what you want, Louisa? You want me to take advantage? To strip away that gown and expose your breasts in the moonlight?"

She gulped as her body reacted instinctively. "I..."

"Then I'll take you down to the pavilion, remove the last of your clothing, and watch your body glow in the lights of the night sky? Is that what you want, Louisa?"

"No..." But the word was a moan, and they both knew it was a lie. "I... The women, Albert," she croaked.

He sighed and tugged away, and she was cold, raised both arms to wrap around herself. "Damn it. They were Frederick's sister and mother, and I didn't know you'd seen them. They said there were two ladies there, but it never occurred to me ... Is that why you didn't ride with me yesterday? Is that why you weren't at home?" His eyes glinted.

"I... Amelia and I didn't know."

He shook his head. "So instead, you chose to dress like a goddess and pull some other poor fool..." he hissed then sighed. "If you want pleasure, Louisa, then look no further. I'm already a damned fool for getting entangled in your web, why not enjoy the spoils too?" She didn't miss the bitterness in his words. "Hung for a sheep as a lamb." Now he reached out, tugging her close. "Meet me tonight by the back fence at two. I'll be there, and you can do as you wish." On those words he released her then spun away, leaving her confused and sorry she'd ever made this foolish plan.

CHAPTER

FOURTEEN

Albert waited by the gate separating the two houses, feeling foolish and pleased no one else could see him. Not that he expected Louisa to join him, not after his buffoonish behaviour. The truth was though, the very thought she might turn up was like a siren's lure.

The sound of waves crashing on the beach below told him time was ticking away, and he checked his watch. Three minutes past the hour. He'd give her a few more minutes before retiring inside.

A creak caught his attention, and he waited as the gate creaked open. Wondered if that might be *her*.

The gate opened fully, and she stepped through the entrance. There in the moonlight she stood. Louisa.

Her long hair was loose, flowing down her back, and he stared, unable to speak for a moment.

"You came," he murmured.

"I…" She dithered, her hands folded together, as if she didn't quite trust them not to give away her secrets. "I wanted to talk to you."

"Why?" He needed to know if she wanted more than just talk. Was she here to follow through on the promise in that gown tonight?

"Because I was hurt." Louisa clapped a hand over her mouth, eyes widening. "I meant..."

"That was an honest answer, Louisa. Tell me what hurt you." His chest ached for some reason.

"I thought... I couldn't believe you'd be squiring another woman if she wasn't somehow of value to you." She gulped and glanced away. "I thought you were like Jeremy." The misery in her tone tugged harder, his chest tightening, and this time he rubbed it, but it didn't ease the discomfort.

"I'm not Jeremy. I'm not even like him, Louisa."

She glanced at him. "I know, but... I want something I don't think I'm ever meant to have." He detected the glint of tears in her eyes.

"What?"

"I want to be loved. *I want to be cherished.* I don't want to have to deal with the aftermath and women like Pamela Jezerey or the whispers from society." She moved, her body jerking as she released the emotions that she'd obviously pent up inside her. The ones he wanted to soothe. "I don't want people watching me to see how I'll handle the latest revelation. I don't want someone who merely wants my funds. *I want to be important to someone.*"

Anguish poured from her words, and he stepped forward, unable to stop himself. He tugged her into his arms as the hunger rose to show her not everyone would use and abuse her. Her arms circled him convulsively, holding tight, and he felt the vibrations of her body.

"Louisa, Jeremy was a fool. I'm not." His mouth descended and he kissed her.

Louisa gasped as his lips touched hers, her body burning with a furious kind of passion. It drove her to open her lips and accept what he'd give. Her fingers clutched at him, finding the material of his clothes, and her mind was overridden by the intense desire to strip him, to feel the firm flesh she knew lay just beneath. To feel like she mattered.

He lifted her in his arms and carried her to the small gazebo hidden from sight by the brushes. Inside he laid her down and God help her! She let him. Let his hands roam while his mouth traced a scorching path down her cheek and neck.

The gown she'd changed into, a pale blue tea gown, was light and easily divested. Once the ties were released, she shrugged the material from her shoulders. It pooled at her feet, then she shifted her attentions and dragged off his coat. His shirt glowed in the pale moonlight as his chest rose and fell rapidly.

"Louisa, stop," he entreated.

His words pierced her, and panting, she tried to slide away from him, feeling like she'd crossed some boundary. She was, after all, half-naked before a man who didn't want...

"Just for a moment," he explained. "It's been a long time, and I want you to enjoy this as much as I will." She looked at his face, saw the way his eyes glittered, and a crest rose over his cheeks. His chest moved rapidly, and she knew he too was just as affected.

"Albert?"

His eyes closed then reopened and she read in their depths understanding of her fears. "Yes, I want you. But I will not rush and rut like an animal. You deserve more. I will give you more."

Now emboldened, Louisa rose. "Then let me." Her fingers shook as she reached around and found the strings of her corset. His gaze watched every move, and she felt the strings giving, the corset loosening until finally it dropped away, and she wore only drawers, stockings, and chemise.

"Such beauty," he breathed and reached again.

Her body flamed when his touch settled at her waist. "But you're still..."

"Shhh..." he entreated. "Let me worship you." His kiss this time was tender, and she gloried in the emotions that now danced within her.

Her fingers tangled in his hair, and she undulated as he laid her upon the blanket he'd laid at some point on the marble bench.

She let him push her down so that she half-lay, with one knee bent upward, while her body ached for his touch. The sea air caressed her flesh as he pulled back. "Albert?"

He was working on removing his shirt, uncovering miles of flesh, and her body shook with the hunger roaring inside her. He flung his shirt to the floor and started working at the buttons of his pants while she watched. She'd never wanted to see as badly as she did now, and when he was finally bare, she couldn't stop her hand from reaching out.

Her fingertip slid against his warm skin while her belly quivered. "Beauty is mine to behold," she whispered, letting her eyes roam over his form, noting the erection jutting proudly.

He moved closer. "I feel that it's still hidden from my view. Come beauty, let me divest you of these unnecessary garments." His hands found the ribbon holding her drawers in place and removed the soft lawn of her underwear, so she finally lay before him, naked and wanting.

The air wafted, with a salty scent, and teased her nipples.

She'd never been bared in the open, but it seemed right for them both as the night wrapped itself around them in a sensual veiling.

His hand cupped a breast. "Your nipples are like raspberries, and I need to taste them."

Then he leaned forward and laid his lips to her breast. Never had they been touched like this, and a flash of arousal shot from breast to loin, tight enough to make her groan. His tongue touched the tip, and she bowed up, aware of the movement of his hand finding her thigh and kneading it before sliding upward, inexorably toward the point that ached for more.

His fingers found the curls hiding her most intimate secrets. "I want to touch you. I want to do so much, but I want your trust too. Do you trust me?" His voice was different, guttural and demanding.

"Yes," she whispered and found she did.

"Then lie back and let me make you feel, Louisa." And he did, his fingers finding the damp folds and sliding within, oh so deep and moving in a way that caused her to want more, to feel the hunger building while nerves throbbed and jumped.

In and out he moved them, while feasting on her and whispering words that were darkly erotic and drugging.

"You feel so wet and ready, Louisa. I know you want me. I want you too. I ache for you. I ache to slide into you and make you mine. Are you ready?"

She arched up and cried out, her body a bow of tight pleasure that finally splintered, while in the distance she heard the crashing of waves.

Long seconds passed until finally she realised he was moving, opening her legs enough that he could move between them. "Open your eyes, my dear. Watch me as I slide into your body. As I pleasure you like no one else has ever done before."

Her lids were heavy, but she did as he instructed, watching his face as he positioned himself. Watched the moment his eyes widened as he slid deep, fascinated in the play of muscles at his cheeks and jaw while his fingers found the nub of desire and slowly, ever so slowly, built the flames of hunger within her again.

"Feel me, Louisa. Know that we are joined. One body and complete." He moved, and she gasped.

"Yes, I feel you," she answered.

His smile took on an intensity she'd never seen before. "Mine now. Forever mine." And he increased the pace, but she kept pace, needing the magic he was sharing with her.

The more he moved, the more she craved and the faster she rocked, as hunger ravaged and burned.

Her body tightened like an overwound spring and at the precipice she closed her eyes.

"Watch me," he demanded, but her body demanded she feel.

She splintered in his arms, and he followed down into the vortex of pleasure. Lost in waves of ecstasy.

Louisa opened her eyes long moments later, while his weight was levered up, on strong forearms. Still joined, her brain told her.

"Albert?"

"Shhh," he whispered. "Just let me be close."

She wound her arms around him and clung, wondering what would happen next, now that she'd thrown caution to the winds.

Her skin started to cool, and as if he read her thoughts, he rose and collected their discarded clothing, assisting her back into the corset that now seemed too tight, too uncomfortable, and rubbed against the skin of nipples and breast that were hypersensitive.

As she dressed in silence thoughts spun around in her head. What next? How could she go back to the dull life she'd grown accustomed to?

"Louisa, tonight was just the start. You know that, don't you?"

She spun. "The start?"

"I don't make love to women and leave them. Not like this. You're... This is different."

Louisa bit her lip. "Different? Really?" A tiny spurt of temper raised its head.

"We will make this formal. Marriage and..."

"And I didn't ask you for that." But in her mind, perhaps she'd been wanting it as the concern she carried melted away. "But if you marry me, you also get all my problems."

"Your problems aren't that great." He smiled. "And I'd take them on."

Sighing, Louisa slumped back to the seat where just moments

before they'd been intimately tangled. "They may not seem large to you, but Pamela J—"

His eyes narrowed. "She's written again?"

Her nod was slow. "The day I saw you and Mr Hollis at the dressmakers."

He sighed and settled on the seat beside her. "Tomorrow... Today, I'll come call. I'll bring Mr Hollis and his sister and mother. I won't ask for a commitment until you know all, but I will be asking. Be prepared. I think Fred is also coming up to scratch with Mrs Cartwright, so she too should prepare herself."

"Oh!" She hadn't spoken with Amelia about what she'd learned, too lost in the thoughts of her own decisions.

"What?"

"Well, Amelia came and went with Isabelle and Elspeth. We wanted to preserve her name."

"But not yours?" His eyebrow arched, and she blushed.

"It's not that... Amelia's situation is different. She doesn't have a name that will protect her, nor has she money, so we decided that a distance might..." In hindsight it sounded weak and unbelievable. "I didn't tell her as there wasn't time tonight. We can discuss it over breakfast."

"And you'll tell her what exactly?"

Louisa felt the scorch of the blush. "Not everything, just about Mr Hollis and his family. The rest is private. Between you and me."

He rose. "You should go home now, and sleep."

Her body felt heavy, lethargic from the intimacies they'd shared, so she nodded, and he led her back to the gate.

"Until tomorrow night, Louisa. Same time. Here."

She stepped through the gate he'd opened and made her way to the house, but when she settled in her bed, sleep took a long time coming, and even then, it was interspersed with memories of what they'd done.

FIFTEEN

Albert settled in his seat, having finished writing a letter to his man of business, Corvings. He'd need to also send to his solicitors in London and would, he guessed, need to discuss the situation with the viscount and Langdon. After all, he'd need their regard for his proposal to Louisa.

Frederick entered the room. "We have a small problem. Someone tried to gain entry to the house last night, or early this morning."

Albert opened his mouth, but Frederick stilled him with a raised hand.

"They smashed a window in the kitchen with this." Frederick produced a large rock, a piece of paper wrapped around it.

Frowning, Albert reached for the missile but didn't take it from Frederick's grasp. "Have you read it?"

Frederick's brow rose. "No."

Funny he'd not heard anything, and neither had the staff it seemed, if only now they were bringing it to his attention. Not that he'd slept, as he'd felt the urgency to begin cleaning up issues with the estate. He needed to clear Frederick's name, and travel to the manor his mother's father had entrusted to him. Much to do, and not enough time to complete tasks before he was able to make his proposal.

In his mind, the situation had crystalised last night at the soiree. Seeing Louisa in the glittering, scarlet gown, acres of creamy skin revealed for his gaze—and others too.

The confidence she'd exuded, along with the image she'd created with the hair, jewellery, and gown... It had taken his breath away for a long moment before his primal instinct kicked in.

"Albert?" Frederick's voice broke through the introspection.

"My apologies. I have a lot on my mind. Pass it here, please."

The rock that had been thrown into the house was placed on the desk before him. Albert picked at the strings, and the paper fell away. The scrawl reminded him of the writing in the ledgers. *Storck.* Damn his eyes! The bastard didn't know when to walk away.

You took wat was mine! Now I get to take yurs!

Albert frowned and threw the message on the tabletop. "We need to increase the security here, Fred. Your mother and sister might be better at the estate, or we could send them ahead to Australia if they've agreed to the plan."

"We've not really discussed it yet, and I'm not sure sending them immediately would be best. I need to book their passage and arrange transport to my property."

Albert nodded, agreeing with his friend's assessment. "True. Too many things could go wrong. Then, I think we send them to the estate. They'll stay in the main house."

Fred opened his mouth, and Albert knew with a high degree of certainty what he'd say, but he stopped him before a word could emerge. "For their safety. They don't have to be in the main rooms if that makes them uncomfortable, there are plenty of others that would be comfortable for them."

Frederick frowned. "But then ..."

"I'm going to have to relocate there soon. Take control of the situation. I've done all I can so far, and other things have..."

"Mrs Lavenwood?" Frederick guessed, saving Albert from making a mess of explaining.

"Indeed. I plan to ask her to marry me." He said the words out loud for the first time to another person, and Fred stared at him.

"I thought you said—"

"I did," Albert sighed. "But..." He shrugged. He'd spent hours in unbridled intimacy with her, and still was surprised at the way she'd responded to him. The way she'd given herself wholly and without any coyness. She'd been... *honest.*

"Well then, I plan to also propose to Mrs Cartwright. I... She's special and she's kind. Her boy is lively and quick as a whippet. I believe she'd accept my proposal as her affections are... engaged," Frederick mumbled.

"Excellent. The ladies deal well together, so as neighbours they'd be able to support each other." Albert grinned and clapped his friend on the back. "We'd best go see the viscount then and see how he's got on with clearing your name, before seeking their assistance in proposals to the ladies."

Frederick cleared his throat. "But what if they aren't supportive?"

Albert blinked. "One hurdle at a time." They had enough of those, with the mess of Storck hanging over their heads.

"One step at a time, then," Frederick parroted. "When do we leave?"

Louisa couldn't settle this morning. She'd decided that to be at home would not be in her best interests, especially if the spectacle of the night before was an indicator. Oh, no one had said anything, but the looks and whispers had been enough. She had to protect not just herself but also Amelia and the children. Her decision to present herself in such a manner, even though it was supported by her sisters, was something she now regretted. Or at least, on one level.

She rose from the seat and paced the room.

"Louisa, it will be fine. It was only a single night, and no one will hold that against you," Amelia offered.

How could Louisa explain without hurting Amelia's feelings? Amelia didn't understand that society wasn't forgiving and certainly not to an outsider seeking entrée. She'd never had any experience, and while Louisa's was limited, thanks to her sisters and their regular correspondence with lashings of anecdotes, she knew more about the restrictions high society placed on women and, more importantly, matrons.

The knock at the door stopped her in midstep, her hands still wrung together. She turned as the door opened and two envelopes were handed over in silence.

The first she knew the instant she noted the writing. *Pamela.* She didn't feel she could cope with it now and slid it onto the top of the desk. She'd open it and read it later. When she was more able and alone.

The other was from Albert.

Louisa,
It is my intent to call on you later this morning. I am also aware
that Frederick plans to call on Mrs Cartwright. I do hope you'll
understand that this is of import.
However, I have business I must attend to first as does Mr Hollis.
We will be there as expeditiously as possible. Mr Hollis' mother
and sister won't be in attendance however.
Please wait for me.
Albert

Her hands shook as she read the missive. Her brain wanted to create ideas as to what he wished to discuss, what was so important that he had to prepare her for his call.

"Louisa?" Amelia queried.

"The Earl will be calling later today along with Mr Hollis. They ask that we await them."

Amelia's face pinked. "Do you think... Perhaps an offer?"

Louisa shook her head. "I don't know... Perhaps for you, but for me? I doubt it. There's never been an understanding. At no time have we discussed—"

"You're not blind, Louisa. He nearly eats you each time he looks at you. He's interested and has been since the beginning," her friend answered. "I've not known either of you long, but I consider myself an excellent judge of character, and if my knowledge is anything to go by, he has plans for you."

*

Albert detested the need to seek permission to marry Louisa. In his mind, they already were betrothed, but given her connections, he needed to ensure he had her family's approval and support, so now, he waited, cooling his heels in the entryway of the viscount's house.

"Your Grace, if you'd be so kind as to follow me. And Mr Hollis, of course." The butler bowed him into the office he'd visited previously. This time the curtains were closed, a fire in the grate, and the rain didn't echo through the room, though it battered at the windows.

Aeddan rose. "Albert. Frederick." He indicated they should settle themselves in chairs, and he took his own seat, then steepled his hands on his desk. "I do happen to have news. Mr Hollis, there was little to no paperwork submitted, which in and of itself is an anomaly. I requested an immediate investigation, and it seems there were some who raised concerns, including the shopkeeper himself. He felt the truth was never made clear and that you were a scapegoat for his lordship. It wasn't the only time this occurred, and as such, I have here a letter from the judiciary which exonerates you from any wrongdoing. A copy has also been sent to the colonial office."

Albert settled back in his chair. "Then that settles that problem and opens a new one."

Frederick cleared his throat. "Mrs Cartwright is an honourable woman, a widow. One I have come to know and regard in these last weeks. I hoped…" He cleared his throat again, and Albert felt for his friend, but this was something only Frederick could do. "I wish to pay my addresses. Ask for her hand, but look for your support first."

Aeddan inhaled. "Your financial position?"

Albert slid a sheaf of papers across the desk. "He's in excellent financial health. I had Corvings draw this up, as I expected this question."

The viscount flipped through the pages, his finger sliding down the lines of figures. "Yes, I can see that. When do you wish to make the request?"

"As soon as… T… Today, if possible," Frederick stuttered.

"Indeed. Then you have my support on the proviso that you make arrangements for her child—" Aeddan urged.

"I plan to discuss his taking my name. He's a good and bright boy. One I would be keen to call my own." Frederick now straightened up and spoke with determination, as if he'd argue Aeddan questioning his intent.

"Fine then. Well, I wish you the best of luck." Aeddan extended his hand and Frederick shook it.

"I also wish to make a request, Aeddan," Albert added, and the viscount turned his gaze on him.

"And?"

"Louisa has engaged my affections. I find her to be a woman who is looking to make herself, one who is honest and true. One who stands by her word. I wish… I intend to present an offer to her, today. While I don't need your approval, for she is both of age and financially secure, I would value your support."

Aeddan frowned. "You do realise that she is her own person? That her fortune is hers to do with as she pleases but cannot be gifted by way of dowry?"

Albert blushed, not liking the line of questioning, yet aware the conversation was necessary. "I have my own money, sufficient to keep Louisa in the style she is accustomed to. I don't want her money, it can be kept for her children for all I care." He shoved the second sheaf across the desk. "As you will see, I have control of the estate, which is seriously depleted, but I fully own my property and a manor which I inherited from my mother. Both of which are turning excellent profits. I do need to make changes to my routine, and as such, it will likely require me spending several months of the year here in England ensuring the estate and manor are well-run. I have other proposals I wish to make, including the purchase of a ship of sufficient size to make the journey from England to Australia in a timely manner. New steamships—"

Aeddan cocked his head. "Interesting. But I think that may be something to discuss with Louisa, Elspeth, and Isabelle. They jointly own and conduct the business of Forster Shipping. It may make more sense to consider proposing that to them, and defraying the costs of cargo shipments and so on." He harrumphed. "I also understand your situation, but this is a hasty step given our last conversation certainly didn't indicate a strong interest in Louisa."

"I have spent many hours in her presence and feel that she is the woman who would be the countess I need, and a suitable mother to—"

"Come, man! She's not an employee," blustered Aeddan.

"No," Albert answered. "She is the woman I would take to my wife, to carry and raise my children. To walk beside me in two very different worlds. She is poised and able, and..." He shrugged, wishing there was a simple way to explain the complex web of emotions that roiled inside him. "She's... She's more."

"Indeed," Aeddan answered. "And the girls?"

"Marina and Eleanora are bright, and I will make every provision for them. I understand their taking my name would not be as easy as in Frederick's situation, but I will care for and love them as my own. I will ensure they're safe and educated, and should they wish to return to London, I will ensure their—"

The viscount cut him off with a smile and shake of his head. "Then I believe you have my support, Albert, not that it's up to me, and once I present your answers to Langdon, I have every faith he too will support your suit. So, there you have it."

Now the deed was done, and Albert and Frederick absented themselves to walk home. Their steps were the only noise as both declined to talk about the interview that had just passed. In Albert's mind, discussing it constituted something akin to tempting fate, so they made their way toward the house and the future he hadn't dared to dream of. The rain had passed, and he was thankful. It would allow him time to think as they walked.

They'd rounded the corner and the sea boiled, the sound filling the silence, when he noted a movement near his front door. "Fred," he murmured. "We have company."

His friend lifted his head, and they both stopped in their tracks.

Albert's focus narrowed now, as if his brain recognised the threat and was ready for action. Muscles tensed as he moved forward with a purpose, Frederick flanking him.

Men came at them, brawny with faces twisted with malice. They grunted, and one called out, "At 'em, lads!"

They engaged, hands and fists seeking their marks, while he and Frederick used their canes to bat away those who strayed too close.

He heard a call go out, but didn't change his focus as one particularly nasty thug sprang toward him, fingers curled like he used them as claws. Albert dodged but not before the sting of something bit deep.

Others joined in, but it was the sound of a scream that curdled his guts. "Albert!"

Louisa.

Primal instinct took over as he shoved and bashed his way toward her, aware that anyone seeking to attack him in broad daylight wouldn't care that she was a woman. They'd use her as a tool. His brain near splintered with rage at the thought, but he was too slow, noting that the man who'd called at the beginning had captured her, and held her arms behind her back.

"Let her go," Albert bellowed while the wild pulse of blood surged in his veins.

"Not until I get what I came for," the man replied, his yellowed teeth on display in the parody of a smile. "And I might just take a taste of this delicious morsel here. Just for meself." The creature laughed and lowered his head toward Louisa.

Just as he made to kiss Louisa, she stomped down hard. The heel of her boot must have caught an unprotected spot on his foot, and he yowled and threw her to the ground.

Albert lunged and caught her close, noting the way her hair came loose and settled in a wild cloud about her shoulders. Strands of gold glinting in the sunlight.

Albert roared and pushed her toward the door. "Get inside," he yelled, and the men, finally recognising their danger, ran. The sounds of hobnail boots smashing down on cobbles rang in the air as they sought shelter far from Albert.

He didn't give chase as the man who'd captured Louisa was hobbling, too slow to escape, and Albert caught him. "Who are you?" The words escaped in a dangerous growl. His entire body shook as adrenaline coursed, his body still wired for action, to protect and to deal with the threat.

"S... Simmons," the man croaked while Albert squeezed his neck in an unbreakable grip.

"And what, Mr Simmons, are you seeking? And for whom?" He enunciated each word clearly, letting the reality of the man's danger sink deep.

"Storck sent me. Said you'd stolen his books. I swear it's just a job." The man's voice quavered with terror, and Albert didn't deny he drew a savage type of satisfaction from the sound.

"Just a job, eh? Grabbing innocent women is a job?" There was an urge to smash his fist into the man's face.

A soft hand touched his shoulder. "Albert?"

Louisa.

"You shouldn't be here, Louisa." It was all he could do to keep himself in check, and right now it was vitally important that she didn't see the fury inside him. She might otherwise refuse him and that... "Gods!" he growled. "Where do I find him? Storck?"

"I aint sure that's a good idea. He'll kill me."

Louisa gasped. "Kill?"

"Aye, missus. He's an angry man, and even more so since the Earl here took what was his."

"I removed nothing belonging to him. He was in my home, he'd stripped the place bare and had his own thugs in place to keep my people from being about their business. He's a thief and a liar." Albert wrenched the man upright. "So, tell me where he is, or I'll call the runners. Have you taken into charge—"

"The Yew Tree, an inn near—"

"I know where it is. Fred, deal with the miscreant. Have the men convey him to the police. I need to—"

"Wait," Louisa called, and Albert stilled, turned to look at her.

"I have to do this, Louisa." He needed her to understand.

"I know. But just... Don't go alone, Albert. If he's sent thugs after you, he's not likely to be alone. Let me send for Aeddan. He and Langdon have connections." Her eyes begged him to listen.

He inhaled then sighed. "Alright."

She flicked a hand and he realised she'd had help at the ready. She'd not waited to be told, or even sent them to take over and save him. No, she'd bided her time, marshalled her troops, and when he was willing, she'd made a considered and valuable point.

One of the footmen ran off, and Albert wondered what she would have done if he hadn't agreed. "Louisa?"

"He's gone for Aeddan. Aeddan will bring Langdon. Now, come inside and let me clean the cuts and blood from your face. Mr Hollis too."

The men looked to him, and he nodded. "Alright, only long enough for the others to arrive."

Mrs Cartwright hovered in the foyer, and he noted towels, bowls of water, and hot tea waited. He allowed Louisa to usher him into the parlor, and he settled in a wing chair while Fred took the other one. Each woman took a bowl and wet cloth and set to work.

Albert hissed as Louisa found forming bruises, and she commented, "dear me," more than once. "You have a couple of nasty cuts, and you're favouring your left side, so I'm thinking you took a hit or two there too."

"I don't need the physician," he muttered.

"No, but you do need assistance. It's clear the situation isn't safe to be out alone." She captured his gaze. "If for no one else, Albert, then for me. Please." He noted the sheen of tears, but she controlled them. "Please, don't take any chances."

❦

Louisa couldn't find the thoughts that explained the aftermath of the attack, only that she didn't want Albert to face this man Storck by himself. It made sense that a man like that, who'd send multiple thugs, wouldn't leave himself open to attack.

So, when Aeddan and Langdon arrived, with Elspeth and Isabelle in tow, she breathed a deep, relieved sigh.

The men conversed quietly, after asking the ladies to give them a moment. The women bustled about settling themselves into their customary chairs and waited. No one spoke a word, and for the first time, Louisa had an inkling of the life her sisters had led before returning home to the safety of England.

"Louisa and Amelia, are you both fine?" Isabelle enquired.

"I'm personally fine, but I'm concerned that Albert would just head off to take on this Storck character by himself. I have no idea what he was thinking!" She rubbed a hand over her brow.

"Louisa was so courageous, and Mr Hollis and the Earl... They were holding their own, but then the men arrived and, I just stood here..." Amelia wailed.

"Nonsense. You had the household marshalled with towels and bowls of fresh water and salve along with bandages, Amelia. You did your bit too!" Louisa was so proud of her friend, the way she'd prepared the household to deal with injuries.

Aeddan and Albert walked over to the ladies and glanced at them. "Everything fine?" Aeddan enquired.

"Oh yes," answered Elspeth. "Just fine. You men go deal with the problem, and we'll wait here for you."

Aeddan blinked. "I'll leave the carriage."

"Oh, don't do that. Simply return once you've attended to your task," she countered and smiled. "We'll wait here and socialise a little."

Albert looked at Louisa, and she had a sneaking suspicion there was something he wanted to share privately, but knew that opportunity was not to be had right now. "We'll be back as swiftly as we can." His hand brushed hers, and those nerves that had quivered and jumped last night did the same again.

"Take care," she whispered, then the men left the room.

"If I didn't know better, I'd say your emotions are involved, Louisa," Isabelle said, and Louisa felt the burn of a blush on her face.

"Perhaps."

"Oh tosh," Elspeth batted back. "I see you watching him, and I see him watching you. His emotions are also engaged. So, what do you plan to do about it?" She cocked her head to one side. "Or was that what the dress and the soiree were all about? Are you hoping he'll come up to scratch?"

Now it was Louisa's turn to blink. "I hadn't really considered it. I mean, he's got his estate and land in Australia. My life is here..." She twisted her fingers together.

"Really? Or is that what you're telling yourself? Is this more about not being prepared to take a chance if it eventuates? What about Amelia?" Isabelle shuffled closer to the edge of her chair and leaned her body forward.

"What about me?" the woman squeaked.

"Mr Hollis is also interested if I don't miss my guess. Is it your intention that if he asks, you'll go with him to Australia? Are you willing and able to give up all this for a man?"

Her eyes glittered with hope. "If he should ask, and I have no idea if he will, then I would need to consider what is best for my son and myself. If it were for love... Then yes. For anything less, no. And Daniel must be considered." Amelia swiped at a tear that escaped down her cheek. "I loved my husband, but he left me with nothing. Louisa has made me welcome and offered me a home, offered protection for my son. I won't jeopardise that."

Louisa took her hand. "If he truly loves you and can make that proposal, then I will support you. If he's simply toying with your feelings though, you'll have a home with me. Daniel will always be welcome too."

Tea was brought in then and the women settled back to wait for the men.

CHAPTER
SIXTEEN

he Yew Tree was a small public house in a township several miles from Brighton, and Albert stared at the façade. It was run-down, with a messy yard and little, to his mind, to make anyone want to frequent the establishment.

"You'll go first," Aeddan reminded him. They'd discussed the strategy on the drive, and it was decided that throwing Storck off, making him think that Albert had come alone, would make him cocky. If he had men, he wouldn't call them all.

"Give me five minutes, then the rest of you come in," he agreed, climbing down from the carriage. He pulled his jacket close and headed for the door.

It gave under his push with a squeak and the near-empty bar quieted on his entry. In the far corner, leaning up against a wall, was Storck. His face a rictus of surprise that quickly passed and was replaced by a sneer. "So, the thief creeps into the hole looking for a prize."

Albert kept his cool and moved forward, keeping the pace of his steps even. "Storck. You and I need to have a discussion."

The man laughed, it was raucous, and others joined in, though it ceased abruptly at Albert's raised brow. "I'm thinking my boys found you. Taught you a lesson."

A smile wreathed Albert's face, muscles twitching into position. "No, Storck. I taught them one, which is why I'm here. I talk. You listen."

"And you're going to do that how? You ain't got no supporters here, no one to fight for you so you don't dirty those pretty hands of yours."

"Is that so?" Albert said, taking a step closer to Storck. His eyes darted to and fro.

Storck clearly thought he had the upper hand, and snarled, "Boys, teach this fool a lesson," he sneered.

Three men rose, and Albert turned to look at them. They were dressed in the uniform of a navvy. Their denim pants were stained and torn, their shirts ripped at collar and cuff, the clothing filthy from their labours. The stamp of their hobnailed boots echoed in the silence.

"Really?" Albert turned back to Storck and smiled.

Storck blanched. "You're bluffing. If you had others, they'd be here, backing you up."

Albert's grin grew wider as the squeak of the opening door heralded his support crew. Feet moved and he glanced over his shoulder. Langdon, Aeddan, and Fred had been reinforced by two of Aeddan's footmen. They'd seen service in the navy and were brawny. Good fighters, according to Aeddan. The five men fanned out, creating a barrier between Albert and Storck's three supporters.

Storck clearly summed up the situation and rose, started inching toward a doorway. *Probably leads through the kitchen to the outside.*

Albert moved, his feet swift, and blocked Storck's retreat. "Now, let's talk, shall we?"

"Ain't nothing to talk about. You took what were mine," blustered the older man.

Albert reached out, grabbed Storck, and dragged him back to the table then shoved him to the bench seat. The three men muttered but Albert ignored them, assured that if they made a move, his men would deal with them.

"You sent men after me. That was a bad move, Storck. A very bad move indeed. See these men," he said, waving a hand at the others. "They've worked for the government. They've done bad things, some really bad things. You crossed me, and that means you've crossed them. Those men make people disappear."

Storck's face lost what little colour he still had left. "You don't..." He licked his lips. "Ain't meaning nothing."

"I was willing to ignore what you'd done, let you go. But you've created a problem for me now. I can't conveniently forget your actions, not when you keep coming for me. And even worse, one of your men attacked a lady. A well-born lady. One connected to that tall man over there." He pointed to Aeddan. "And that other one too," he added, including Langdon. "That was a bad mistake."

"I ain't..."

"Now, now, let's talk honestly. You thought you'd what? Blackmail me? Bleed me dry? Make me pay?" Albert leaned against the table. "I'm not going to give in. You took money from the estate and other items of value, and that can't be ignored. So, here's your choice — my men put you on a boat to the Americas, you never come back."

Storck's mouth dropped open.

"I'm not interested in prosecuting. Oh, I can and will if you don't accept this offer, but you don't want to do that. I promise you. We..." he stated, indicating the others, "have connections, and we'll use them. You go and take your men with you. Or you face the assizes."

Storck made to rise, his ire clear to see. "You cain't make me..."

Aeddan cleared his throat. "I have friends in high and low places. Friends who'll make you disappear. *Is that really what you want?*"

Storck dropped back into his seat. "My family..."

"Will be much better off without you. Or you can send for them once you've established yourself in America. If you take this opportunity, our men will see you to a ship," Langdon offered.

The door opened and more of Aeddan and Langdon's men

entered, and Storck watched as they took hold of his men. The man deflated before him, the bluster melting away as his chest sagged.

"We go, boys," Storck muttered. But in his eyes, Albert saw fury warring with the knowledge he'd overreached.

The new men who'd just entered rounded up Storck and his three thugs, then pushed them toward the door, but not before Albert heard Storck mutter, "You bastard. I've other men—"

Aeddan moved in front of the older man and smiled. The flash of his eyes, the sudden harshness of his face, and the sheer muscular bulk dwarfed Storck. "And if they move against our friend, the Earl here, or his family or any of his property, we'll know. And the friends I send next time won't be as forgiving," Aeddan added, and the man dropped his head and was ushered from the building.

The sound of carriages had Louisa straightening in her chair. Elspeth had retired upstairs for a small nap, and Isabelle was in the garden with the children and Amelia, so Louisa was alone for the moment.

She rose and headed for the window, watched as Aeddan, Langdon, and Mr Hollis climbed from the carriage. She scanned the area and noted a horse and recognised the form astride it. *Albert.*

The butterflies in her stomach started to subside, having taken flight the minute the men had left, and she placed her hand flat against her belly. "At last," she breathed.

She rang the bell as the sound of the door opened. The parlour door was next, and she scanned each as they entered, searching for signs of injury, but there wasn't anything new.

The maid appeared and Louisa gave instructions for the women to return and a luncheon to be put together in the dining room.

Albert slid around the knot of men and took her hand, lifted it to his lips. "Forgive me, Louisa."

"I..." The women bustled into the room, and though Louisa made to move away, Albert held her hand in his grasp.

"Gentlemen, if you would give me the room for a moment?" Albert said.

Aeddan smiled. "Of course. But be quick about it. We'll move to the dining room."

Louisa blinked at the strange way Aeddan had agreed, but watched in silence as they trooped from the room, the door closing behind them.

"Albert?"

"Storck has been a difficulty for me since my return to England. Now that he has been dealt with, I'm in a position to ask for your hand."

The words, alien and unexpected, settled inside her, but the thing she wanted most wasn't what he was offering... was it? "Why? Why do you wish to marry me?"

Albert stared. "I'd say it's pretty easy to understand, after last night."

She bit her lip. "So, because last night we engaged in—"

"Because last night I showed you that I want to be with you. That I... I need you like no other man does. That you and I fit together."

Her hands twined together, nails bit deep into flesh. "What if I didn't want... I'm not sure..."

"And if a child resulted from last night? What then?" He growled. "Louisa, I can offer you my name, protection for your daughters. We work together, and people have seen the connection between us."

"So, you want to marry me because society expects it?" Her voice rose.

"No, Louisa. What do you want me to say? I love you? I don't know that. But I can say, you'll be supported. You'll be safe. I'll be honest and I won't stray. You can travel, or if you want to take a more involved role in Forster Shipping, I'll support that. I want children. I have the title and I need a wife and an heir."

Everything he said was true, and she liked him. Even more, last night had opened her eyes to a level of intimacy she'd never experienced with Jeremy. She'd felt closer to Albert and... Maybe that was all she could look forward to? She'd never met another man who'd treated her like the centre of his world. Not really. She could accept his offer of marriage. She could make the leap and—

"Louisa? Please be my wife." He tugged her close. "Let me love you every night. Carry my children and help me run my estates. I can't do it alone, and no other woman feels as right as you do."

As far as proposals went, it wasn't romantic. Not like Jeremy... He'd brought chocolates and flowers, recited a poem as they'd walked through her mother's rose garden. She'd had stars in her eyes and had squealed when he'd asked. This time was different. There was a gravitas... But it was a chance. An opportunity. A new chapter, and all she had to do was accept it. Her brain spun; her psyche urged her to accept, but she couldn't understand why that was the reaction. Her stomach knotted...

"Yes," she breathed. "I will."

❧

Lunch was a subdued celebration. As they entered the dining room, Albert noted Frederick and Mrs Cartwright sitting beside each other, their fingers entwined. "You asked?" Albert enquired.

"Aye," Fred answered with a smile. "She accepted."

"Very good. I also asked Louisa."

Isabelle and Elspeth stopped chatting and stared. "Pardon?" asked Elspeth.

"And?" urged Isabelle.

"I accepted," Louisa said beside him.

Congratulations flowed around the table, and Albert settled in beside Louisa. The housemaids tittered and left the room, returning moments later with a bottle of champagne.

"Excellent," Albert said, waiting as the glasses were poured and handed to the eight gathered around the table.

"When?" asked Elspeth, and Louisa frowned.

"I've not yet had time to think..." she answered.

"Soon," Albert interposed. "I'm thinking, unless you'd wish otherwise, we can be wed from the estate. We'll ride out there tomorrow if you'd like and you can inspect the house. I need to meet with the tenants and make arrangements. You can decide if you wish to redecorate the countess' suite."

"What a grand idea," cooed Isabelle. "We could make a party of it."

"Stay for a few days and explore," beseeched Elspeth.

"I can meet Frederick's mother and sister," added Amelia.

"Yes, what a grand idea," Louisa agreed, though she appeared a trifle overcome by the speed with which decisions were being made.

"The children should come. Is the nursery up to scratch?" Isabelle enquired.

"I'm not sure, but that is an excellent point. When I return home, I'll write a letter and send it to the Hall. They may need to bring in some assistance."

"Perhaps then, we should give the staff a few days' notice so they can prepare. Say three? That way they can clean and lay in provisions," Louisa suggested. "I can prepare the children with Amelia." She tugged her hand from Albert's, and he frowned.

Even worse was the sound of disquiet in her voice. Did she regret her hasty decision? He wasn't offering love, but he'd been honest in everything he'd said and in his offer.

It wasn't quite the celebration he was expecting, but he shrugged and made a mental note to craft a notice to be sent to the papers in London. After all, the sooner they all knew she was taken, the sooner anyone else with designs on Louisa—or, more of a concern, her fortune—would be given notice.

CHAPTER

SEVENTEEN

TWO DAYS LATER

The missive was lying on the salver when Louisa descended the stairs in the morning. She was coming to learn that gossip moved quickly in society's circles.

So, you brought him up to scratch. An Earl, no less. That means
you have the wherewithal to settle your debt with me. I'm not
greedy. Five thousand should be sufficient for my needs.
You have one week to make the payment, or I will make known the
results of your husband's straying. Won't that be nice? The future
countess and her dead husband's by-blow.
P

Her stomach roiled, and she scrunched up the letter. "What am I going to do?" she moaned.

"Louisa, you have to tell him." Amelia slid her arms around Louisa. "This isn't something you can keep a secret. He needs to know. He can stop her, so you need to let him help you."

139

"But what if she's right? What if I can't birth a son?" It was the one thing she feared above all. Albert had mentioned the need for an heir, and though Pamela hadn't presented Jeremy with a son, it made Louisa question her ability. Albert might change his mind, and that thought had her stomach knotting even further.

"Really? You're going to let that woman ruin the chance you have at happiness? The Earl loves you."

"No, he doesn't. He said he didn't know if he did."

Amelia sighed. "Men don't think about their emotions, and they certainly don't talk about them. But think! He rode with you every day, would wait. Those days you didn't ride, when we thought they'd strayed, he looked for you. He's not just attentive, but listened as you talked about the children. He's... If he didn't love you, do you think he'd have chosen a wife who already has children?"

"I..." Her mind spun. Amelia was saying things she desperately wanted to believe. Could she...? Louisa laid the letter on the table.

"Did you tell him?"

"Tell him what, Amelia?"

"That you love him? That you were hurt when you thought he'd found a mistress? That you sparkle when he enters the room. That you watch him?"

Amelia's words were like jolts. "I..." Everything she'd said was right. The attraction was there, the fears that he'd find her less. That she wanted to be with him. That his lovemaking had awakened something deep inside her. Was that really love? "I don't know, Amelia. What if I'm wrong again?"

"What if you're right?" Amelia let go of her, picked up the letter and read it. "You need to talk to him. Explain. Let him help you. While you refuse to do that, you're only giving him part of yourself. That's not how a healthy marriage begins."

No, otherwise in many ways, she'd be no different than Jeremy. Hiding part of herself wasn't fair or right.

Albert was due to visit this morning, and she settled herself in the chair to wait, though 'settled' wasn't the appropriate term, she thought.

When the knock came, she bolted upright.

"You don't need to work yourself into a panic," Amelia soothed as she handed Louisa the letter. "Show him."

Albert entered the room, and Louisa gulped down a breath.

Amelia rose. "I'll leave you two alone for a few minutes."

Once she'd left, Albert frowned. "Is something wrong?"

Louisa thrust the letter into his hands.

He scanned it and growled. "You've only received one or two others, do you know..."

"I've received dozens."

He stared at her. "Dozens? You've never said that. Tell me."

She shivered and moved to the desk, opened a drawer, and removed the sheaf. Thrust them at him. "She's been sending more and more with increased regularity. This one was here this morning. I don't know how she gets them here, not one of the staff have admitted..." She cocked her head to the side. "I asked after they started arriving here. At home, they were shoved under the door, so that was explainable. But here..."

"Has she been here? In Brighton, at events you've attended?"

"Yes. Quite a few, including the one where I met you first. I can always feel her eyes on me, and sometimes even when I'm sure she's not at an event, it feels like she is. I don't..." She licked her lips. "I don't know how to address this. I don't believe paying her is an option, because she's the kind that will only be emboldened."

"I would agree." Albert took her hand and towed her to the settee. "I'll talk to Aeddan. He'll know—"

"No. I don't want Aeddan to sort it. I just need advice..." She needed to know how to stand on her own two feet, to be strong and take charge. Since Jeremy's death she'd been relying on her brothers-in-law and sisters for assistance and advice. She'd only just begun to find her own way in life.

It also occurred to Louisa that even though she'd be married, and her life would be melded to another's, that it didn't mean she couldn't still learn to stand alone. To make decisions about what she wanted in life. A man didn't have to strip those newly emerging skills from her. She may have only known Albert a short time, but she hoped he'd support her need to be strong and independent. He'd already said he would support her if she became more involved with the shipping line. He'd said all the right things...

"If you don't want me to approach Aeddan, then we'll have to come up with something ourselves. We have time, tomorrow we'll travel to Cimmaron, and we'll have time. You'll have space to think, and my people will police anyone entering the estate."

She stared into his eyes and nodded. There was something both soothing and captivating about his eyes. The same as the way that when he wound his arms around her it was like being enveloped by peace. She closed her eyes.

"You don't have to do it all alone, Louisa. I'm here and will support you. I don't want to smother you or control your life, but I do want to know. I want us to be equals in the marriage. Once we travel to Australia, you'll need to help me. The large properties are best maintained by couples who work together. We'll need to travel back here too, regularly. I can't simply walk away... and I'll need your assistance."

Warmth flooded her chilled limbs. Hearing him talk about a partnership, equality... He had no idea how much that gave her the strength to tell him what she needed and wanted. "I know that's not a conventional marriage, but I look at Isabelle and Elspeth. Theirs aren't conventional marriages either, but I see how well they work together with their husbands. Like two sides of one coin. I mean..."

He cupped her cheek. "I know. I've noted it too."

Turning her head, Louisa kissed his palm. "I want more, Albert. I don't want to be tied to a role that has been cut by other wives. I want to explore and do." She let the words die away because it felt... *fast*. Yes, they would marry, but that didn't mean that she could be forward in how she talked to Albert. She glanced under her eyelashes at him.

He smiled, the glitter in his eyes she thought very much a reminder of their encounter several nights before. "I sent word that when we arrive at Cimmaron, you'd be in the countess' suite immediately. Eleanora and Marina, along with Daniel and Nanny, will move to the nursery. Amelia and Fred will take the rooms nearest them, and your sisters and their husbands will be accommodated in the guest wing."

She read the subtext. He wanted them to be able to be alone. Unlike here, where the house was too small for Amelia to not know, or Frederick, they'd be able to continue their intimacies if they both wished it.

"I'm pleased," she answered and blushed.

He rubbed his thumb over her cheek and leaned in, the heat of his breath whispering against her lips, and a languor spread throughout her body. He was like a drug, veiling reality so all that existed was a sensual world.

The creak of the door had them springing apart. He scowled, and she muffled a tiny laugh at his expression. "Soon," he muttered under his breath, and though her body tingled at the thought that very soon they'd be able to hide away, for now she had to simply try and quell the primal hunger that gnawed at her.

Leaving Louisa's home, Albert once more considered the missive he'd seen. Dozens. Had no one thought to look deeper? To ask questions? He made a point that he would find out more. Send for information. Corvings would know how to go about it, because Albert knew bringing either Aeddan or Langdon into the situation wouldn't assist his cause.

CHAPTER

EIGHTEEN

Louisa and Amelia, along with the three children, waited as their carriage rounded the corner and trundled through the gates. Albert had warned her the house required extensive refurbishment, but he'd already sent men to begin work on the hedgerows and gates, and she saw signs of their efforts. Here and there mounds of greenery pointed to the work they'd already completed, removing overgrowth, limbs had been trimmed. The hedgerows had men working at coppicing, but she knew it would take years for the efforts to show properly.

The gates themselves needed painting, and she found herself wondering at the colour that would best show the coat of arms that was wrought into the iron. The path was clear, though badly needing ruts repaired, as the carriage jounced up and down.

"Mama? Why are we bouncing?" enquired Eleanora.

"The Earl said that the property needs a lot of time and work, my love. It's not been a priority for his family, but now that we're coming to live here..." She glanced at Amelia.

"He wants it fixed so everyone is safe. But look out there, Ellie! You'll be able to learn to ride in all this land."

They'd cleared the woods, and a large, verdant green lawn led to a house. Impressive in style, but she could see the façade was clearly in need of cleaning. To one side the remains of an ivy mask was being pulled away from the blocks. *That's a good thing, as ivy is so invasive it'll penetrate the mortar.*

The windows gleamed, and the gardens were dotted by men working to repair the neglect of years. A fountain sat in the middle of the drive, only a dribble, but even here, the bones of the design were clear.

They drew up outside the entrance, the grandeur marred by remnants of lichen between the steps, as the horses the men rode stepped restlessly until they dismounted and handed the reins to stablehands. "My word, there's still much to be done, isn't there?" Amelia said.

"Yes." But for all that there was to do, Louisa felt a thrill that she'd be able to have free rein to bring the house back to life.

They climbed down from the carriage, and through the doorway Louisa could see the assembled staff waited. She entered the building, on Albert's arm, to the shuttered faces of the men and women. For a moment, Louisa felt disquiet, until the children wandered in, and then it was as if a change came over the staff. Eleanora took her hand and Marina tottered along, as one by one they were introduced to their 'future countess' as Albert called her in his address to the staff.

An older woman came forward. "I'm Mrs Coombs, the housekeeper. Madam, I do hope your tenure here as countess is joyful."

"I'm sure it will be, Mrs Coombs. Now, before I do anything else, could someone take Nanny and the children up to the nursery, and perhaps, Mrs Coombs, you'd show me to—"

"His Grace has asked that we prepare the countess' suite for you. I'm happy to escort you," she added. "'Tis been a long time since it's been occupied. After the master left, the countess travelled to London and stayed there."

Louisa heard the hurt. "I'm sure that's made things difficult for you. I'd be interested in discussing the staffing and so on."

"Aye, that would assist a lot, madam."

Louisa wasn't sure she liked being termed 'madam,' but perhaps in time they might be inclined to call her Miss Louisa as the majority of staff at home still did. "Then lead on, Mrs Coombs."

Albert nodded, as if he too were pleased with the interest she was taking in the place, but before he could speak one of the staff caught his attention and he turned and followed him away.

Louisa climbed the steps behind the housekeeper, noting the state of the carpet runners showing signs of use, with exposed threads and holes. The walls were faded, and the many portraits looked down at her, she fancied, like they wondered who the interloper was.

"This part of the house is newer. Only built some hundred years ago. Some of the oldest parts are several hundred years in age. The previous Earl wasn't inclined toward the upkeep of the house. He closed sections up, and no one has been near the ballroom in nigh on fifteen years."

"Indeed," she answered, squirreling away the information.

Chairs and tables were polished to a sheen, but they were also looking old, and she made a mental note to begin working through the house, room by room, and discuss things that needed to be addressed with Albert. He'd already indicated he had no problems with her renovating, but the sheer magnitude of work surprised her.

"And staff? You have adequate for the house?" Louisa asked.

"Well madam, the Earl has indicated we may need more. Said as how you'll be here for some of the time and travelling to Australia at others."

"Albert has a large property there, and it also needs his regard. It is our plan to split our time between the properties here and to travel there on a rotating basis."

"Mrs Hollis and Laura will also be relocating, I was told. To the colony where Mr Hollis has land," Mrs Coombs said.

"I believe so, but Mrs Cartwright may have a better idea of when and how, as she is to marry Mr Hollis. But Albert... The Earl said Mr Hollis has a property, a prosperous one alongside his."

Mrs Coombs sniffed as she opened a door. "I haven't ever heard of such a thing as the head gardener's son being accommodated inside the main house."

Understanding the situation was so far removed from Mrs Coombs experience, Louisa smiled. "I think times are changing, Mrs Coombs. Now, is this the countess' room?"

"Indeed, madam. This was her sitting room, while through here was her boudoir. She always kept it immaculate like, but the late Earl didn't really care. He had it locked up. We've dusted and aired, but the furnishings are in need of attention."

Louisa looked around the room. It was showing signs of neglect, the soft furnishings faded, and curtains showed their need for replacement, some with threads hanging down. But the room itself was pretty, with walls covered in ivory moiré, and deep carpets of a pale blue. She stepped into the boudoir and took in the mossy covers of the bed, the curtains to match, and the large fireplace with two deep chairs and a small table.

"It's lovely. Just needs some new, soft coverings," Louisa murmured.

"You don't wish to change the colours?"

The surprise in Mrs Coombs' voice had Louisa turning. "No, the colours are very restful and tasteful. Yes, there is work to be done, but nothing that cannot be carried out by local women, I believe, when it comes to the soft furnishings. Come, show me the bathing room, then I'd like to visit the nursery and check on the children."

Dinner was over and the party was breaking up for the evening. Albert's pulse quickened, because Louisa would be in the countess' rooms. Would she welcome his advance? Would she open her door?

He stripped and slid into the robe he'd arranged for one of the men of the house to lay out for him. The nonsense of a valet was not for Albert. His father and his brother's valets had both been dispensed with. Garbutt, his father's man, had been retired, and Albert had been made aware that the man had been offered a small cottage on the estate. Rayston, his brother's man, had sourced alternative employment, so that was one thing Albert didn't need to worry about.

Perhaps he needed someone to care for his wardrobe and Louisa... His thoughts turned to the woman he knew was on the other side of the connecting door.

He raised his hand to knock then stopped. Would she welcome him tonight? The thought was a refrain, and he turned around and spied the brandy on the side. There was only one glass, but his mind conjured up a scene.

Albert scooped both bottle and glass up and returned to the door, knocked, then opened it.

He noted the startlement on Louisa's face. "Oh!"

"I thought perhaps, a brandy with me?"

"Please come in," she said.

He didn't miss the way she blinked rapidly, or the up-and-down movement of her chest. Her hands fluttered in the air. Neither did he miss the fact that her night attire was a floating froth that had his imagination working in overdrive, along with a growing need in his body. His loins ached for her, but he'd need to step carefully.

"I'm not sure if you've had brandy before?"

"I... No. I mean, Jeremy did, but I never..." She shrugged.

"I know Jeremy was your husband, but from the little you've

said, he didn't treat you as an equal." He waited for the words to settle in her mind.

Her smile was small but grew as she unwound the intent behind his words. "No. I was young, and he was so… male. My aunt reinforced that I was a female and needed a man. Someone strong and brave, and charismatic. To my mind, he was all that and more. I believed he was everything I wanted. Then I learned about him, the demands he made. He knew what was in my dowry, but I think he never thought I or my sisters would stop him from accessing the funds of the estate. My sisters are clever women, in case you didn't know it."

Albert slipped the glass and bottle onto the small table before the fire. "They are clever, but they aren't you, Louisa. Not who you really are. You're brave and strong too. You accepted that fate for a woman and a widow meant being at home, until you chose not to any longer. You were the one who planned the trip to Brighton, and you're the one who knew what she wanted…"

Her soft laugh stopped him. "I wanted more, but I needed time. I had to publicly grieve, and that was difficult. By then I knew him — who and what he was. His mistresses, and let me tell you Lady Pamela wasn't the only one. Housemaids and farmers' wives also numbered. I… I had to parade before them in black. I had to pretend for two years to be diminished, but I knew the truth at his funeral." She stalked back and forth, the froth of her nightrail billowing. "I listened to his family extolling his many virtues."

She spun back to him, her eyes bright with remembered pain, and Albert moved beside her. "I promise you now, there will be no other."

"How? How can you say that, standing here before me? I would have believed that of Jeremy… I did!" Her hands flew into the air.

The pressure in his chest, the one he tried so hard to ignore whenever they discussed her deceased husband, pushed harder. It was like a block that he needed to shove aside. "I promise because you're the woman I want."

"He said that too, Albert." Her lips drooped and she stepped nearer, cupped his cheek. "I want to believe you. I want to be important to you in a way no one else can ever be. I want to matter."

He groaned and turned his head, kissed the palm of her hand. "You do. I feel things with you I've never felt before. I don't know what it is exactly, but it's deep and honest, Louisa. Don't misunderstand that. I won't misrepresent my feelings, but if it's love, when I know it for that, then I will say so. I won't lie. I saw my father do that for years, and it destroyed my mother — maybe not physically, but emotionally. I swore when I was young that would never be me. I stand by that."

"Then pour me a brandy, Albert, and we'll talk. Just..."

"Just what?" He waited as she hesitated.

"Let's not talk about Jeremy tonight." She gathered the thin layers of cloth about her and settled in the seat by the fire.

"Alright then." He poured the liquid into the glass and turned. "Sip slowly," he instructed, handing the glass over. "Your apartments meet with your approval?"

Now she smiled. "Yes, though the soft furnishings need cleaning and some replacing, if you're amenable?"

"The house needs a woman's touch," he said. "It's been a long time since anyone took any real notice, and I'm more than happy to leave the interiors to you. Funds will be tight for the estate for some time—"

"Then perhaps I might use some of the funds I have available—"

"I won't allow you to sink your money—"

"Shhh. Trust me. The funds I've held for the last two years will more than adequately see to the refurbishment. As to the rest..." She shrugged. "I've been thinking. If you're travelling between Australia and England routinely, you won't be the only one. I've often thought a steamer might be useful for Forster Shipping to cut the travel time. We can do more runs, carry more cargo. As an owner, I would be able to use the ships for travel, as would you."

He stared at her. "Have you discussed this with your sisters?"

She twined her fingers now that she'd returned the glass. "Not yet."

Not for the first time, Albert realised how little she'd previously been involved in the company. "You want to become more involved?"

"I... As I've grown older, I understand just how much my sisters protected me from. Business vagaries and life. But I'm not a naive girl anymore. I have children to set an example for."

He nodded, and a sudden vision popped into his mind. Louisa large with child, her body changing, and the dappled light of a billabong hidden from view, her spread on a blanket and naked. Needy for his touch.

"Albert?"

He gulped the brandy and set the glass aside. "I will leave you now," he said, but the look on her face, the way her lips turned down, stopped him from rising.

"Did I say something wrong?" Her whisper tore at him, and it took him a moment to reconcile the strong woman who'd laid with him in a gazebo to this one. These were the two sides of the same coin, and she was allowing him to see her vulnerabilities. Opening herself emotionally.

"No, Louisa. I had a thought. A vision if you will. One that one day I fully intend to make good on. But if you want me to stay, I will." His voice rose and she smiled, once more shyly.

"I'd really like that."

L ouisa couldn't hide her body's reaction to Albert's nearness. The way she felt hot and needy. Empty and ready for his caress. When he suggested he stay, it had been all she could get out to banally answer, "I'd really like that."

This time, when he stood, he held out a hand. "Come, I want to show you something."

His fingers were warm, but she accepted the touch and let him assist her up.

He led her to the wall, and she waited as he pressed and touched until he breathed out, "There it is."

The panel slid aside.

"This was built during the war of the roses," Albert said. "It's said a much earlier countess—I'm not sure which—wasn't a royalist. Her family was loyal to Cromwell, and though she loved her husband and adored her children, it was necessary for her to hide until her husband could proposition the crown for a pardon." Albert grabbed a candle and held it aloft. "Come with me."

She followed him into the walls of the house, and along a corridor. "Where does this lead?"

He smiled. "There's a folly in the garden. My mother used to take me there when my father and brother were raging. Before I left, it became quite a regular occurrence."

"Things weren't easy for you, were they?"

He shrugged. "We all have our problems, mine just happened to be my father and brother." They made their way down a small flight of stairs until they reached a hidden door. He slid a hand into his pocket and withdrew a key. It ground in the lock, but the door sprang open. "Come."

Exiting into the garden, an overgrown mass of weeds, Louisa gasped. "A walled garden…"

"Turn around," he whispered, and she did.

A small turret rose, obscured from the house by a small copse of trees. "Can we go in?"

Albert shook his head. "Not yet. I want to be sure it's safe, especially now that there are children in the house."

That he'd considered Marina and Eleanora warmed her insides further, and she moved to him, his arms opening as she pushed into his embrace and settled her lips to his. "Thank you."

"I will do everything I can for you and those girls. And any others we might beget."

The words penetrated her being, sinking into her bones. "Children?"

"I'd like at least two. Maybe three, if you're willing."

She felt her smile melting away. "A son."

He cursed, and once more she was overwhelmed by a sense of helplessness. "She's wrong," he whispered. "But I don't care. There's a distant cousin if we only have girls."

"But you need an heir," she whispered against his lips.

He tugged back, took her shoulders in his hands, and she felt the strength of them, and when his gaze captured hers, she felt the weight of his words too. "I. Don't. Care. Louisa, you aren't a broodmare I chose because you can give me the child I need. If we have children, they'll be wanted and loved. Don't you think that's more important?"

Tears burned in her eyes as she nodded. "I do, but I also know you're an Earl."

Albert growled. "I told you I have a cousin. If all else fails, he will become the next Earl. I'm not marrying you for a son. Come close, feel the way my body responds to yours, Louisa. That is why. The feelings inside me, the ones I don't know how to name, are the reason. Because I know you're strong and—"

"Because of that night," she whispered while a sense of helplessness cascaded through her. She dropped her head away, not wanting to read the truth in his eyes. *He regrets—*

"No, Louisa. I wouldn't have been with you if I hadn't felt a connection, but if I had..." He stopped and demanded wordlessly that she listen, waited until her gaze settled on his face. "Damn it all, Louisa, if I hadn't felt what I do, I would have walked away after I'd enjoyed the dalliance. With you... it's more."

"Show me," she demanded, suddenly needing him to prove his affections.

He pulled her to a seat, hidden until now, and set the candle down. "Come here, Louisa." The huskiness of his tone pulled at strings hidden within her body, and a flash of heat shot from breast to loins.

She followed him, wondering how his words could drug her so efficiently. "Albert, I..."

"Shhh..." It was his turn to quiet her words as he placed a soft finger against her lips. His hand dropped then, moving to the ribbon closure of her wrapper. "Such a pretty piece of fabric, and yet it hides something so beauteous." His fingers plucked before pulling on the bow, and the material slid open.

"Ohh..." she whispered as his fingers pushed on one shoulder of the gown, sliding it so her shoulder was bared under the moonlight.

"Your skin is like velvet. The most perfect velvet ever created. So soft and needing to be treated with the utmost care." His head dipped toward her skin, a spot she'd never before considered erogenous, at least not until Albert. One kiss, then another, then more dotted her shoulder, and though she wanted more, he didn't touch any other part of her.

"Albert, I want more," she whispered as nerve endings sang.

"In due time," he replied, and his fingers found the other side, slid the material from her shoulder, and the gown fell to the floor. Forgotten.

Now he stepped behind her. He placed his hands on her shoulders, and she shivered, not from the night air, but the sensuality of his movements, the way he cupped both shoulders then slid his hands down her arms. His lips found the nape of her neck, and she arched as his hands covered her breasts, lifted them slightly.

"To me, you are the most beautiful woman in the world. It's not just how you look or how you dress or even how you act, it's your heart, Louisa. Watching you with your daughters and Amelia's son. Watching the way you never make Amelia feel less than a close friend."

"Ahh..." she uttered, but he cut off her words.

"Frederick is so thankful you set the tone for society to accept him and Amelia. For me, though, it's the way you are you. Giving and soft, yet determined to be your own person. To stand alone, even when you don't have to. That's the woman I want to spend my life with."

The words, whispered against her ear, filled her with hope.

She bit her lip as another groan tried to break free from her throat, his hands moulding the flesh of her breasts and gently plucking at the nipples, while heat scorched her from the inside.

"Albert..." Need was coursing, and the veil of eroticism had settled over her brain. "Come to bed with me," she muttered. She bent and retrieved her gown, slid it over her nakedness.

"I will," he answered. She gasped as he lifted her into his arms, then carried her back to her room. "Tonight we'll rest in a comfortable bed, and I'll show you some of the many ways I want to pleasure you."

Once they entered the bedroom, her gaze met his, and she gasped again at the intensity in his eyes. She cupped his cheek. "I want this, and I want you. I ache for you, Albert," she said, and he smiled darkly, so her insides curled into knots of erotic need.

She slid from his grasp, and stood before him.

"Take off your gown," he muttered and settled himself on the bed.

"What?" She blinked.

"Remove your gown for me, so I can look at you."

A blush seared her cheeks. "Strip?"

"Please."

She gulped, but without releasing his gaze, she found the buttons and slowly, achingly, released them. But before the gown fell, she slid her hands up, holding the material in place. "I want you to do the same. Strip for me." She'd never before been so bold or made a demand of her lover, but he grinned.

"Of course, my dear." Albert pushed off the bed, and his hand moved to the sash at his waist, tugged, and the dressing gown gaped, and she knew he was naked beneath. Her mouth dried, because she now saw the evidence of his desire, jutting out. "I'll remove mine, when you remove yours." There was a seed of humour in his voice, mixed in with hunger.

"I…" She released the cloth, and it dropped away as he shrugged out of his covering.

Embarrassment filled her. Her breasts were just a little less firm than before children, her hips a little wider, and her stomach… Last time, it had just been the glow of moonlight, where tonight he could see every dip and hollow and curve of her in the gaslight. Her hands rose instinctively.

"Don't," he whispered, took her shoulders, and turned her. The looking glass she'd used this evening to dress with now became a sexual tool. "Look at yourself." His hand cupped her breast. "See what I see. A beautiful woman. Ripe and hungry. See how your body flushes. My hand, dark and large, on your breast. The way your nipples call out for me to love them. Suckle at them. Or watch my hand on your belly. See how your chest rises."

She was melting at his words, need coursing deep.

"Watch my hand as it roams over your body. Watch your eyes when I kiss your neck." His mouth slid against her skin, hot and slow.

Her knees wobbled.

His hand roamed further and found the thatch of hair at her sex, combed the hairs apart, then slid further. Deeper until he found her hidden lips. "Now watch as they dive into you, Louisa. Feel the heat I find and how ready you are."

One finger delved into her, and she cried out. "Albert!"

"Not yet, my sweet. Let me seek a little more."

But she couldn't. The drumming of her blood and the wire inside her were too tight, too close. It was too much. Her eyes closed, and a shattering climax erupted.

Moments — long or short, she didn't know — passed before she realised he must have lifted her and carried her to the bed. Her body felt heavy and replete, and yet there was another need brewing.

"Albert? I've never…" She couldn't finish the sentence.

"Tonight, once won't be enough, my love." He kissed her, the depth and ferocity dragging her back into the world of emotion and need.

His erection poked at her, and she opened her legs.

"Not yet, sweet Louisa. Soon." Once more, his hand found the space between her legs. "There is so much more than simply me sliding within your body. Pleasure should be shared. Given and taken. Put your hands on me. Feel me."

Touch him. How? Her hand reached out, fingertips grazing his chest. Heat radiated, and his breathing came quickly. A nipple, dark and hard, stood out from the hairs on his chest, and she had a sudden urgent need to feel it. See if it was hard or soft. She slid her fingers closer, and he laughed. "Oh God, yes!"

Emboldened, she covered it.

He hissed, and she pulled her hand away, but he gripped it, returned it to his chest. "You're not hurting me. It's just... I feel the pleasure of your touch. I want it so much, and I want to be in you... Sometimes control is a mere thread."

She stared. "I make you feel like that?"

He grunted. "Feel more and find out." Now he gripped her wrist and tugged it down, cupped his cock. "See?"

"I didn't know I could do that. I..."

"Unless I ask you not to, I'm as much an open canvass to you as you are to me. There will be times, usually when I'm close to the edge of my control, I'll stop you, but simply because waiting any longer, feeling your touch, will push me over the edge."

"Oh."

"Now, let me do something new. Lie back." His hand pushed her flat, and she let go of him, allowed him to set the pace.

His lips found one nipple and sucked it into his mouth. She cried out and didn't stop him. Couldn't. He suckled, tongue laving the tip before letting go with a tiny pop, then blew on the distended point.

The pleasure had her arching up again, and he laughed. "You need more though." His mouth slid down to her belly, and she watched between half-closed eyelids. He swiped his tongue over the swell. "One day, this will be big, and I'll talk to the babe within you." His fingers found her centre again, and she jerked her hips up. "Just getting ready," he whispered, and this time he slid further down.

"What...?"

"Wait and see, my sweet Louisa. I want to taste you now." And with his gaze firmly on hers, his hands opened her, and he settled his mouth to her.

Her eyes closed as pleasure built, unfamiliar sensations while he lapped at her and sucked. Tasted. Feasted.

The hunger that rose was a raging torrent when he lifted away. She opened her eyes and saw him wiping his mouth while his body lurched up, no grace in his movements. His cheeks were tight, and his eyes glittered in the light. His erection was hard and pulsing, and she wanted it and him. Right now.

She shifted her hips as he settled himself, then with a single, smooth slide, he penetrated her.

Her hard nipples grazed his chest as he grabbed her close, the kiss hot and frenzied, and she tasted her essence on his tongue. It swept aside any kind of urbanity and propelled them forward. Their bodies moved and fingers gripped as they both needed more, racing toward an orgasm that crashed down, dragged them under the waves, and left them shattered, entwined, and breathless.

Their hearts beat rapidly as he held her close, and just as she allowed sleep to carry her away, she was sure he spoke.

Albert held Louisa close and gave in to the knowledge he'd been trying to avoid. He'd fallen in love. The woman he would marry and who would carry his child was the woman he loved above all else.

"I love you," he whispered, aware she was asleep, and he took a moment to be thankful for the woman in his arms and the depth of the emotional tie he felt. It was a monumental discovery, and one he'd never expected to make. He would have settled eventually, taken a wife, and had a child or two. They'd have dealt together creditably, while he focussed on building a life for his family. He hadn't expected more since he'd left the estate all those years ago.

Now, he was the Earl, with an estate to save, his mother's inheritance to oversee, and a property. Two little girls who would become his daughters once he wed their mother, and a wife. A woman he liked and admired, a woman who wasn't content to merely be a wife and mother. She wanted more too. She wanted to be strong, to stand out in a world where being meek and biddable were highly prized.

Of course, there was much to arrange now that she was here. He also had two surprises in his bedroom.

The first was a marriage license he'd obtained the day before. He felt a sudden need to finalise their marriage sooner rather than later, so he could settle to the task of bringing the estate back to a functioning property.

The second? He'd sent to the manor after receiving information from the steward. Much of his mother's jewellery, the pieces his father hadn't been able to dispose of, had been returned to the home of her childhood. He'd remembered one piece in particular. Not one of the ones he'd received in the letter from his mother, but a small topaz ring. He remembered it from childhood and the story she'd told him about it. It had belonged to some long-dead aunt who had loved a man, but he'd been killed in a war before they could marry. She'd worn it for the rest of her life and had never married, because she'd loved the man she'd lost so much.

Albert wanted that connection with Louisa, so he'd sent for it and hoped she'd wear it as a token of his... love.

He closed his eyes, the tumult of today and the realisation wearing him out. He'd rest a little. When they both woke, he'd tell her.

❧

Louisa woke slowly, as layers of sleep rose from her mind, to find a warm and heavy body beside hers. She'd nestled in, her breasts nudged against a man, and the hairs of his chest tickling her nose.

"Oh," she breathed.

"Good morning, Louisa."

She sat upright. "Albert?"

He grinned. "Now, that's a sight I'm looking forward to seeing for the rest of my life."

She looked down and noted the nakedness of her chest and reached for the coverings, but he stayed her hand.

"No. I like the view," he stated.

She blushed deeply. "It's not seemly."

He sighed. "What we do, as man and wife, so long as we both agree and enjoy, is more than acceptable, Louisa. But if I do something you find uncomfortable or don't like, you only have to say."

She blushed harder and her skin burned.

"Have I done anything that makes you uncomfortable?" He leaned in, waiting for her to reply. "Louisa?"

Shaking her head, Louisa whispered, "No. Surprising and unusual, but not uncomfortable."

He dragged her into his arms. "Good. Then say good morning to me, so we may start our day."

"I... Good morning, Albert."

His smile had her guts melting once more. "Excellent. Now, much as I'd love to stay here and enjoy a pleasurable morning, we have guests. We should join them for breakfast, then I'd like to talk to you in private."

Louisa frowned. "It's private here."

"No. Fully dressed, in my office. Then I need to meet with Aeddan and Langdon. Frederick too. And you'll be busy. Very busy."

His words were confusing, but as she opened her mouth, he silenced her by kissing her deeply until the now well-known fog descended on her mind. By the time she dragged herself free, he was out of the bed, around the other side, and scooping up his dressing gown.

"I'll see you in the breakfast parlour soon, Louisa."

As he opened the adjoining door, he looked back, winked, then disappeared from sight.

Albert waited impatiently once the breakfast had been consumed. Now he paced the office, dreading and excited to share the news of the special license he'd procured. Thanks to Langdon and his connections, it had been arranged easily enough, but Albert asked the man not to share the information with his wife, lest Isabelle told Louisa.

The door opened, and Albert turned, watching as Louisa entered the room. Her gaze took in the heavy, dark furnishings, and he wondered what she thought of it. For himself, his awareness of the room and the changes wrought left him unsettled. He knew there were books missing, tomes that detailed the financial history of the estate. Where would he find them?

He noted missing pieces, small decorative items, including a small marble bust his grandfather had acquired in Egypt. Also missing was a silver pen his mother had given his father on their marriage, in a crystal box lined in ruby velvet.

"My father's office never looked like this," she breathed. "The room was smaller, and the book collection along with it." Louisa ran her fingers over a shelf of the bookcase that lined the walls.

"This area was expanded by my grandfather during the last major extension to the house." His grandfather had worked hard to build up the estate, and it had only taken a single generation for everything his grandfather had amassed to be squandered.

"I know you said the finances are thin, but the bones of the house are strong, Albert."

Her words were a reminder that not everything was in a poor state. They could rebuild, and with the right people and careful choices, they would survive this latest hiccup.

She turned. "You wanted to talk with me?"

He indicated she should settle into a chair, and waited as she did. He swallowed as his nerves concerning the matter he was about to discuss with her grew.

"Albert?"

He blinked. "Yes. I wanted to raise the matter of a wedding."

Oh, she mouthed. "I hadn't really thought about it, not yet. I wasn't quite sure how to start the preparations given the circumstances."

"Excellent." He turned and moved to the window and looked out. "I don't wish to take a long time. From my perspective, the sooner we're wed, the easier it will be for everyone."

"I... Yes, I believe you're right. When were you thinking then?"

He rubbed his hand over his head and turned back. "You have the gown already?"

She stared at him. "Oh... Well, I do, yes. Isabelle, Elspeth, Amelia, and I felt it was wise to have it made up immediately."

"Good. If there is no one you wish to invite, I'd like to have the marriage finalised tomorrow." He waited and watched her. She stilled and stared at him.

"I... I have no one I'd wish to invite. Everyone who is important is already here. I'm just wondering with regards to the marriage contract?"

"I had planned to meet with Aeddan and Langdon later. Normally we would have a solicitor draw up the agreement, but I believe since the situation is clear-cut, we could simply draw it up, sign it, and send it off to my solicitors, who will hold it in their files. To be clear, I have no intentions of accepting funds from you or from Forster Shipping. My mother's manor will be kept separate from the property of the Earldom, which is entailed in perpetuity. Your funds will remain your own, and your portion of Forster Shipping will be kept for your daughters, Eleanora and Marina."

"You've taken a lot of pains to ensure their inheritance is protected, but any children we might have will receive—"

"I had hoped you'd agree that the manor should be their inheritance. I make the distinctions in the understanding that their father left them and you with no funds at his death. Am I correct?" He hated dismembering their future in such a cold and unemotional way, but it was necessary ahead of time, so everyone knew and agreed.

"No," she whispered. "I mean, that's right."

"Once Aeddan and Langdon are available, I'd like you to attend, so we can be clear as to what we've all agreed to. So, with the wedding, are you in agreement that we shall continue toward a swift marriage?"

Her hands were clasped together, but he didn't detect any negative emotional response from Louisa.

"Yes. But I'd like two days at least. I would like to see the chapel and I think meet with the staff in preparation. There won't be a large breakfast, but I do believe there should be some kind of celebration. I'd also like to prepare Marina and Eleanora ahead of time, as this is a major event for them."

These were things Albert hadn't considered, and though she'd had the large wedding before, according to Aeddan and Langdon, he also didn't want to strip her of the opportunity or pageantry she deserved.

"Of course," he responded. "I hadn't considered the children might see this as a significant change."

Louisa smiled. "Have you had much to do with children?"

"Some of my staff have families. I spend time with them," he added, but accepted the intent of her words in good humour.

"Ahh. I see. Well, I suppose you'd best spend time with the girls, so they know that you're interested in them and their future." She smiled. "But two days should be sufficient. And yes, I'd appreciate being involved in the discussion with Aeddan and Langdon."

"Excellent. Then I'll send a letter to the local vicar today requesting his assistance." He settled into the seat.

"Albert? Is there anything or anyone you want in attendance at our wedding? Your heir, perhaps?" She leaned toward him.

He shook his head. "No. We will need to send an announcement to *The Times* afterward, but there is no one else. Frederick is here, and to be honest, the only other people who I would want are here on the estate." He cocked his head. "You don't seem overly concerned about the speed?"

Her brow lifted. "Should I? We've already been intimate several times, and that was an aspect of the reason behind our marriage, Albert. But I've also been married before. I had the gown and the celebration, and it didn't make things right. It didn't improve the outcome. The only thing I'm concerned about, given our discussion, is that you don't feel short-changed."

He laughed. "It was never my intention to marry, Louisa. Or if I had, there wouldn't be the attachment I feel."

Her eyes widened. "Attachment?"

Albert sighed. He wasn't yet ready to disclose just how attached he was, but he felt it was important to make some kind of declaration. "I made no secret of the fact that I find you interesting. You're a beautiful woman, and I desire you. I enjoy talking with you and spending time together."

A eddan and Langdon entered the room, Albert watched them and noted when they realised Louisa was also present. "You needed our assistance?"

"I asked you here, with Louisa present, to assist with the writing of an agreement between Louisa and myself ahead of our marriage. I need someone to draw it up, to ensure it's fair to Louisa and her daughters and to any further children we may produce. Louisa's current holdings remain hers and should be inherited by her daughters at a later date. I have my mother's manor, which I would keep for any children we produce. I do not wish to have access to any funds of Louisa's for the rehabilitation of the estate or the manor. It is hers alone."

Aeddan nodded. "And if the manor were to fail?"

"I have the years to ensure that won't happen. It's in a very strong financial position, and my man, Corvings, prepared a report when I inherited the Earldom, which I am happy to hand over for your perusal. Corvings is—"

"We deal with Corvings ourselves. We are aware of his abilities," Louisa explained.

Albert nodded. "Very well then. Gentlemen?"

"I can draw this up," offered Langdon. "I've some experience in drawing up contracts."

"Thank you." He didn't know if there was anything else, so he waited.

"I'll start work on this immediately, and since it's very clear-cut, I should have it finished in a few hours. May I avail myself of your office?" Langdon asked.

"Indeed." Albert stood as did Aeddan and Louisa. "Louisa and I are going to visit the nursery, then I am meeting with the new steward."

The party trooped into the hallway, and Aeddan stopped Albert.

"I'd be most interested to join you when you ride the estate. I've some ideas, and I'm sure you've got some I've never considered. I too have an estate which could do with some modernisation," Aeddan said.

"Then I'll send for you later. Now, if you'll excuse me, Louisa and I are to visit with Eleanora and Marina." Albert took Louisa's arm, and they started toward the steps.

CHAPTER

NINETEEN

Louisa woke slowly. In the early morning hours, she lay in the bed, aware of the feeling that something big would occur today. It was like a veil had settled on her mind, or a fog, and she needed to clear that away before reality could control her thoughts.

Today, she would marry Albert.

Excitement fizzed through her. "Albert, the Earl of Conney." Later today he would become her husband, and she'd be his countess. Funny, even when she married Jeremy, there'd been pleasure but not the bone-deep sense of change and destiny.

Unable to remain still, Louisa cast the covers aside and moved to the window, opening it and looking out into the yard below. The sun hadn't yet risen, and there was a chill in the air, as winter would soon be encroaching. Amelia and Frederick would also wed today, he'd also obtained a license, and Louisa was pleased to see her friend blossoming with Frederick's adoration.

Her mind turned to Albert. The man was determined to make things happen. Already he'd hired a new steward and the tenants' needs were being catalogued and addressed. Albert had ordered new breeding stock for the cattle so necessary to the livelihood of everyone. He'd ensured the staff knew that any direction she gave had his backing, and he had requested a tour of the house with both her and the housekeeper, so she'd know the true state of the house.

She'd met with staff two days ago, after spending time with Eleanora and Marina in the nursery, and they began the planning for their wedding breakfast, which was now well underway. Louisa had taken great pains to include Amelia in the planning.

Now there was no more to do.

A knock at the door caught her attention. "Come," she called.

The woman who Isabelle and Elspeth's maids were mentoring as a dresser entered the room. "Ma'am, it's time for your breakfast, then it's a nice, hot bath before we begin dressing."

As the dresser slid the door shut, Louisa enquired. "Someone is attending to Amelia?"

"Yes, ma'am," said Jones. "Millie is ensuring her needs are being addressed."

Jones would work well enough, especially once they travelled to Australia. She was young and eager for adventure, unlike Louisa's previous maid, Yates. For a moment Louisa thought back to her wedding to Jeremy. There'd been an excitement with the fuss of gown and preparation, but she'd had no real idea what would occur. Yates had been there, dressing her hair and preparing her clothing. Lousia wondered what Yates would have said about Albert, but Yates been much older — the nursery maid when Lousia had been younger. "She wouldn't have wanted the travel," Louisa murmured.

"Ma'am?" Jones queried.

She smiled at the maid. "I'm just thinking out loud. So, where would you—"

"The footmen have set up a table before the fire in your sitting room, and while you eat, I'll prepare your bath, so you may bathe before dressing."

Louisa entered the room and looked at the table set up before the fire. The table had been laid with immaculate white linen and dishes covered with domes. A pot sat beside the cup and saucer, and she inhaled, the aroma filling her nostrils, and her stomach gurgled.

Settling herself, she lifted off the domes and handed them to Jones then served herself a tasty meal of bacon and sausages, scrambled eggs, tomatoes, and some toast. The pot contained hot chocolate, and she smiled, then set to breaking her fast.

Once she'd eaten her full, she waited for Jones to return.

"Ma'am, if you're ready?"

Louisa rose and followed the woman to the bathing room, and she disrobed. She settled into the highly fragranced water and allowed her mind to still. With her eyes closed, she inhaled and exhaled, letting her body relax fully, until Jones roused her.

"Ma'am? It's time for me to begin with your hair."

"Oh, yes," Louisa answered, well aware that the time for calming her mind was over. Now began the process of preparation.

Albert paced in the office. He'd long since broken his fast and bathed. For now, he wore his suit, sans jacket, ahead of his wedding. Glancing at the clock above his desk, he noted the time as not yet eleven in the morning. He had another hour before he needed to be at the small chapel, but it felt like time was dragging.

Frederick entered the room. "I'm looking for some quiet, and thought you'd be in here. Mind if I join you?"

Albert indicated to the chair opposite. "Your mother and sister are preparing too?"

Frederick nodded. "Your countess-to-be gave direction that they should be attended to as well. Mother is slightly apprehensive, but Laura is enjoying every minute of it."

"They leave tomorrow, am I right? Isabelle and Elspeth had their man organise their passage. They'll be well cared for."

"Aye. I sent word to my man, and he'll meet them on arrival in

Moreton Bay. They'll be transported to my property and await our arrival. Amelia has been preparing Daniel, so he's got what he needs for the journey. We should be able to leave within the week."

"I'll miss you, Fred, but you, Amelia, and Daniel need time to get to know each other. The journey will give you that time."

L ouisa looked at Amelia as she entered the suite, in her pale pink gown, moulded to her figure, with a small comb in her hair detailed in shining stones, her face a wreath of smiles. "You look lovely, Amelia."

Amelia grinned. "I might look lovely, but you are positively gorgeous. That ivory and powder blue makes you look like a goddess."

Louisa touched the careful decorations of blue which Amelia mentioned and turned to the mirror. Not for them the orange blossoms of young brides, nor the whites, but instead they'd chosen colours that enhanced their natural tones. "I'm rather pleased with the design." It too moulded to her body, her golden hair swept up into a chaste roll, secured with sapphire and silver hair combs Isabelle had lent to her.

Elspeth stepped up and handed over the box containing the topaz pieces Albert had sent up for Louisa. The ring on Louisa's finger twinkled as she opened the box, and the stones glinted in the light. "Help me, Elspeth?"

Her sister removed the necklace and fastened it around Louisa's neck, then Louisa added the earrings, and lastly the bracelet.

"It's time, my love," Isabelle called.

The bell was pulled, alerting Nanny that they were ready for the children to arrive, and Louisa considered the day. So much was different, and unlike last time—she made herself a promise that no longer would she allow thoughts of her previous wedding to make their appearance—the wild excitation she'd experienced was replaced with a quiet joy.

"I'm ready," Louisa said.

The brides both accepted bouquets of roses which had been grown in the gardens, they were joined by stephanotis flowers and were formed into balls, to be worn on a ribbon from the wrist.

In a nod to the weather, they each were draped with a fine silk shawl, gifts from their respective husbands, Amelia's in shades of ivory and silver, while Louisa's was a pale blue match for her gown and ivory. The children entered the room and were stilled by their nanny just inside the doorway, and their eyes widened as they took in the two brides.

"Mama! Your gown is so pretty," enthused Eleanora.

Marina squeaked excitedly in her two-year-old voice, "Pwetty!"

Daniel blinked at his mother. "Very pretty."

"Come now, children. Take our hands, and you'll be in the carriage in front of the brides and their sisters," called Nanny as she and the nursery maid waited patiently.

"I want to go with Mama," Eleanora pouted.

Louisa smiled. "Not this time, my love. Stay with Nanny, and afterward, you can travel with Albert and I." They'd already arranged for Albert and herself and the girls to travel in one carriage and Frederick, Amelia, and Daniel to have the second, which she knew would be gaily decorated.

Now they stepped forward, the children preceding them as they made for the stairs which led down to the foyer. They arrived at the doorway and watched as the children and their escorts climbed into the first carriage, decorated with flowers and greenery. After it drove off, then the second, an elaborately decorated landau, arrived before them. She and Amelia were settled first then Elspeth and Isabelle joined them, and with a small jostle they were off, en route to the chapel nearby.

The arrival at the small building built of stone and well-weathered had them pulling to a halt. Dozens loitered by the door, and the women waited for the footmen to open the carriage door. One by one they alighted, with Louisa the last to step down.

Whispers abounded, and Louisa looked at her sisters who smiled then stepped within the building. Amelia was next, and lastly, Louisa stepped inside. The light dimmed, but it was immaculate, cut flowers decorating the pews.

Louisa inhaled deeply then followed Amelia to the aisle, where she saw the two bridegrooms waiting. Frederick looked fine in his fitted suit of black with a pale figured waistcoat, but it was to Albert she looked. His grey suit, white shirt, and the waistcoat of blue were heavily embroidered, and when she looked to his face, his smile was wide. Welcoming.

She began the walk.

❧

Albert blinked and looked at the two women walking toward him. Elspeth and Isabelle, Louisa's sisters who he was coming to know. They wore gowns of bronze and yellow and smiled as they passed him and took their position in the front pew together with the three children and their nannies.

Beyond he caught sight of Amelia in her pale pink gown. "Here's your bride," he muttered to Frederick.

"She's beautiful," he answered.

Then Albert stilled as Louisa entered. *Stunning* was the first word to come to mind. Her gown was ivory and picked out in blue, and with her shining gold hair decorated with a silver and blue stone comb, she appeared like a goddess, stepping down from Mount Olympus. His tongue swelled, and he wanted nothing more than to scoop her up, show the world she was his. Instead, he waited. Impatient to claim her as his wife. In his mind, she'd been his since the moment she'd met him in the garden. This was merely a formality.

There was no music, there hadn't been time to find someone to play, but as the women began their silent trek down the aisle, he knew they didn't need it. There was an air of expectation in the building.

When Louisa reached him, he took her hand, and she smiled at him, her eyes glinting with pleasure, and the air in his lungs expanded.

They turned as one to face the vicar who began, "Dearly beloved…"

L ouisa barely took in the words. Albert was holding her hand and they were pledging to meld their lives together. The gravity of the situation wasn't lost on her, as she struggled to concentrate because suddenly it was real and happening.

"Do you, Albert Michael James Cimmaron, take Louisa Elaine Lavenwood to be your lawfully wedded wife?"

Louisa jolted as the vicar questioned Albert, who smartly answered, "I will," in a loud voice.

"And do you, Louisa Elaine Lavenwood, take Albert Michael James Cimmaron to be your lawfully wedded husband?"

She gulped and looked the older man right in the face. She took a moment, and nodded, before responding, "I will."

The vicar continued the service, repeating his questions to Frederick and Amelia

Rings were produced and one slid onto her finger. She felt the weight of it, after removing her previous one soon after Jeremy's death, once she'd become aware he'd made a mockery of their vows. She'd eschewed any jewellery on that finger until Albert had presented the topaz, but this? While it might be a simple gold band, it signified that they'd both agreed to something deep and rich. The solemnity of the moment had tears burning in her eyes, but she blinked them away, because this was a time of joy, and she'd shed far too many tears in the last few years.

Once they'd finished the formalities and signed the register, they turned together and left the chapel, well-wishers streaming behind them, calling out 'congratulations.' As they exited, petals were flung up and she laughed with the sheer pleasure of the moment.

Albert turned toward those gathered. "Thank you for your wishes today. My wife and I are overjoyed to share this event with you."

"Thank you," Louisa added before the girls came running up. Albert swung Eleanora up while she captured Marina in her arms, and together, they turned and climbed into the waiting landau, its top pulled down, and she noted the feather crests the horses wore. A celebratory finish to match the floral decorated vehicle.

The driver clicked his tongue and flicked the reins, and the horses pulled away to a flurry of cries of 'hurrah.'

"Mama, does this mean Albert is our new papa?" Eleanora's words made her smile.

"Yes, my love. Albert and I and you and Marina are now one family."

"Good," Eleanora said. "Can I call him Papa?"

Louisa glanced at Albert, who now grinned and answered, "I'd really like that, Eleanora, and you can be my big girl."

Eleanora giggled.

CHAPTER
TWENTY

They entered the foyer, and Albert watched as Louisa goggled at the sight of all the staff lined up, dressed in their best uniforms.

Mrs Coombs stepped forward, a joyful smile on her face. "Allow me, on behalf of the maids, to welcome you home, countess. It is our pleasure to serve you."

The butler bowed low. "On behalf of all the staff, we congratulate you both."

Eleanora slid between Louisa and Albert. "What about me?" she squeaked, and the household stilled as if holding their breath.

The butler bent down low. "And you Miss Eleanora, and Miss Marina too."

Albert couldn't contain the guffaw that rose. "Well, there you go, Eleanora, and you too, Marina. Now, I think Nanny has something special planned for both of you and Daniel in the nursery." He handed them over, pleased that Louisa stood by and nodded her agreement. There'd be times he might accidentally overstep, but he hoped they were on the same page in terms of today's efforts.

"That was well done, Albert," she murmured.

He nodded and took her hand and led her to the dining room, the doors opened before them, and he heard her gasp. "Oh my!"

The room was certainly resplendent. The long table set with silver and crystal while a magnificent pineapple graced the centre. Plates of fine white bone china were illuminated by the candles on the table, as the flames jumped and danced, and the chandeliers were also lit.

As they settled to the table, the others filed in, taking their seats, and a merry lunch ensued. Finally, only the cake remained to be cut. It was small but perfect, a dark fruit cake dressed in white icing and intricate flowers. He wondered for a moment how many hours of sleep Cook had got, as he guessed the work to decorate must have taken many hours.

Once the cake was cut and the pieces distributed, their guests, those not staying at the house, left, until finally it was only family in attendance. He and Louisa rose, and they all moved to the parlour to finish the festivities.

Aeddan strode up to Albert, cradling a brandy glass filled with the aromatic spirit. "You did well. No one expects you to hang around, so if you plan to abscond with your bride, you'd best do it now. The staff will attend to our needs."

Albert bowed. "Thank you. Then we shall make our departure, and we'll meet with you all in the morning for your mother and sister's departure."

He stepped away, caught Louisa's eye, and though she blushed, she excused herself from her sister and took his hand. Without a word, they stepped through the doorway and headed for the stairs.

"They're all imagining what we're going to do," she whispered as they ascended.

"Then good for them, but now I want time alone with you, wife." He steered her toward their private apartments, far from prying eyes. Once they reached her door, he stilled her. "I think we can ignore the limitations of yours and my rooms today," he said and pushed the door wide.

She entered, and he followed. He closed the door firmly and tugged her close.

"You looked so lovely today," he said. "And I must admit, this last hour has dragged. I wanted to have you to myself, to feast upon the vision of you. Now I have you here and all I want to do is remove that beautiful gown and show you how much I cherish you."

She gasped as he took her mouth, the kiss gentle as he sipped at her lips, letting her feel the need that was burning inside him.

Her hands clutched at his shoulders, and as he pulled away, she whispered, "You looked most handsome today. I felt wanted, and when you answered Eleanora's question, it melted me." She shook her head. "And that is woefully inadequate, but I'm lost for words. Your sweetness toward her..."

"It's easy to be sweet to both your girls. Both *our* girls," he corrected himself. "I want to raise them beside you. To raise our brood, because that's what they will be." He pulled her toward the bedroom. "But for now, we're alone together. There will be few interruptions, only later a cold collation will be delivered, but tonight is solely for us, wife."

Every word Albert spoke, every action he took for Louisa and her daughters reminded her of his devotion. It made her feel strangely off-kilter, like she was ignoring the single most important thing. How she felt about her new husband. Emotions roiled, and until now, she attempted to ignore the one high on her mind. Did she love him? She wanted him, sexually. She welcomed the partnership he offered, the companionship, but it was so much deeper.

Listening to him talk of their children and their future, it hit like a bolt. Caring for him was such a shallow term. This... This was love. Deep and abiding.

They didn't yet have an association of years, and he hadn't prettied up their courting phase with empty efforts. Everything he'd done had been honest, and that was the key, wasn't it?

She let him pull her into the bedroom, aware of what was to come while a curl of heat rose in her belly, the flame one he'd fanned every night since they'd located to the estate.

Every morning, except this one, he'd risen from her bed, leaving her replete and whole and very much aware that she was valued. She stopped in the doorway as he headed toward the large bed.

An urgency filled her. "Albert?" She needed him to know the truth, the one that couldn't be contained any longer now that the blinders had been stripped from her mind.

He turned in her direction, one brow lifted.

"I love you." The words slipped out, but she held his gaze, hoping he'd read the truth of her declaration. "I wanted to tell you that. You might not reciprocate—"

Any vestige of civility melted from him, instead before her stood a primal male, nostrils flaring, with fierce hunger in his eyes. "Good. Because I love you too."

She blinked. "You do?" Shock coursed deep, replaced by hunger and a strange form of contentment. Love. A small word, but with the tentacles of an abiding connection. Urgency to show him just how much he meant bloomed, and she knew the instant he read that in her facial expression. "So, what comes next?" she asked in a whisper, dipping her eyelids just enough to hopefully appear coquettish.

Albert stalked toward her, his hunger clear. "I've loved you for some time, I was simply waiting for the right time to tell you."

"And here I am, Albert. Yours."

The curl of heat turned into a raging fire, and she wanted him, needed to show him with every ounce of her being just how much he meant to her. They came together, lips colliding as his arms wrapped around her waist. Her body came alive, needing the touch of skin-to-skin. The kiss wasn't enough, and she mewled.

He dragged himself away and wolfishly demanded, "Then I need you naked and beneath me, wife. Because tonight, I plan to show you the many ways you please me — not just sexually, but in every way."

Louisa gulped, suddenly shy as his words excited her. Her fingers moved into her hair, removing the comb, and she stepped to the dressing table. In the mirror she watched as he moved behind her and his fingers, so *damned* clever, found the cunningly hidden buttons at the back of her gown.

"You're truly the most beautiful woman in the world, and I'm the luckiest man," he whispered against the nape of her neck, and she shivered, feeling the benediction of them soul-deep.

"Albert, love me," she whispered, the words broken as she gasped for air. Needing him, desiring his touch. Body melting and brain unable to put together coherent thought.

"I will do that and so much more, Louisa. I burn for you. My nights are constantly plagued by memories of your response to my touch, and I wake up hungry. You've seen that."

As her gown fell to the floor, he slid his hands around her breasts, fingers working at her nipples that already jutted hard and proud. Between her legs, the insistent throb pulsed, and if he didn't love her soon, she'd just die, she thought.

She attempted to turn in his grasp, but he stilled her. "Not yet," he panted. "I want tonight to be different, to last forever."

She groaned. "I won't last forever, and I doubt you will either, Albert. Please," she entreated, then twisted so she faced him. "Let me." Her fingers found his coat and divested him of it. He reached to help, and she laid her hand on his arm. "No, let me tonight."

Albert balled his hands, and the fact that she had this effect on the man standing before her filled her with power. She reached up, onto the balls of her feet, and kissed him quickly, so she could show him she knew the effort this cost him.

Once she subsided, her hands went to work, removing his cravat then flicking open the buttons of his shirt, and she lifted the fine cotton away from his bronzed skin. Not for the first time did she note the difference in tones. "You're darker than me," she said, her pale hand lying against his chest.

When he looked down, he exhaled, but the unsteadiness of it wasn't lost on her. "I ride miles and work in the sun. It's not an easy life, but it's rewarding."

"I see that." And she did. Over the weeks of conversation, he'd told her of the mountains they called the Blue Mountains, a barrier which had only recently been overcome, allowing for expansion of the former colony. He'd told of the privations and unwelcoming wildlife, snakes and kangaroos, spiders, and other deadly creatures. But tonight, they weren't important. The only thing to consider was them — Albert and Louisa.

Her hands found the fastener for his pants, and when they dropped to the floor, she couldn't help herself. "My, only for me," she murmured.

He squirmed. "Perhaps so, but hurry up or I'll expire," Albert growled.

She giggled and glanced up. A mistake.

Albert's hands clamped on her waist and lifted her, carting her to the bed where he laid her down. "I can't wait any longer, Louisa. Have pity."

His hands finished stripping himself as she fumbled with her undergarments, the bedding twisting around her as she hauled at her corset. Then he was there, loosening the strings until he pulled the material away and assisted with her disrobing.

Finally naked, she gazed at him. "You are truly a beautiful man," she whispered.

He didn't answer with words, instead his eyes ran over her nakedness, every glance a touchless caress that quickened her breath. Then he descended — slowly. The kiss was cataclysmic, as hands moved and fingers dug deep, looking for purchase on slippery skin.

She arched and sighed, while he feasted, his hands roaming over her body.

When he nudged her thighs apart, she moaned, because inside her the emptiness ached so much that only he could complete her. As his body slid into hers, she cried out, and he grunted, fingers holding onto her hips that just needed to move.

"Still, Louisa. Be... Still." His words were an entreaty.

Then came movement; faster, wilder, and untamed. Hearts beating frantically as the orgasm loomed.

"Love me," she called out.

"Forever," he vowed.

Then together their bodies splintered, and time stood still as the ultimate act of love played its finale.

Opening her eyes sometime later, she gazed on him, his eyes closed as he held her tight, their bodies still joined. "Thank you," she whispered.

"No, Louisa. I thank you. I never expected this joy. Or to be married to a woman I love and admire so much. I never expected a family of my own, or to feel complete."

Tears pricked, because how could she offer him more when he'd spoken the most beautiful words of all?

CHAPTER

TWENTY-ONE

Morning came far too swiftly for Albert, but he roused Louisa and they rose. "I need to go dress," he muttered regretfully.

She nodded, following him to her sitting room. "Yes, and I need to dress too. Mrs Hollis and Laura are due to leave by lunch, aren't they?"

Albert nodded. "They need to make it to their first stop tonight and will be in London tomorrow evening." He sighed. "We should hurry." But his feet wouldn't move further. It was as if his entire life was here, and he reflected ruefully, it really was.

"Go." Louisa fluttered her hands, as the knocking on the door began.

He left and closed the door between the bedroom suites, his clothes gathered in his hands. He thrust his discarded clothes to the chairs at one end of his bedroom and stalked to the dressing room beyond, tugging out his less formal clothes.

Today he'd need to ride the estate again, and perhaps Louisa might join him? He'd broach that with her after breakfast, but first they had to farewell Mrs Hollis and Laura who'd agreed to travel ahead of them. She'd carry packets from both him and Frederick for their staff, explaining their new status and also directions to follow until arrival. Not that Fred and Amelia would stay long with them now.

Frederick had stated just yesterday that he felt the need to get home. Daniel needed to be settled, and he and Amelia needed time to establish themselves, and besides, he'd been away for several long months, and they'd be due to shear by the time he arrived home. It was an important time on a sheep station.

Not for the first time, Albert wondered if Louisa understood the lack of rainfall or the fine, red dirt was her future, not verdant hills where the sheep grazed here in England. She'd seen some of the colour plates in books, but it didn't really explain the vast emptiness that drove some people wild.

He'd need to spend time with the children too, explaining the dangers and ensuring the nanny and governess he'd already started to consider necessary for Marina and Eleanora would be strong enough to watch out for the safety of his daughters.

It took time to dress, finding clothes that were suitable to farewell Mrs Hollis and appear at the breakfast table, and yet also suitable for the visitations he'd planned. Finally ready, he descended the stairs and entered the breakfast room. Most of the visitors had left, and he settled down in his chair, coffee in hand and a plate when Louisa hurried into the room.

The chatter around the table ceased almost instantly, and Louisa blushed then excused herself to fill a plate before taking her place at the table as the chatter resumed.

Mrs Hollis had chosen to sit near Albert and reached out to touch him. "Thank you for looking after my boy and seeing him settled. His Amelia is a lovely woman, as is your Louisa. You've done well with her."

"I've always been close to Fred. When my father sent him away—"

"I know." She dabbed at her eyes. "It was a terrible time."

"I did what was right, not just because he's my friend, but also because my family wronged him, on so many levels. I'm just pleased his father had no knowledge of this." Indeed, Fred's father had passed away only months before the trumped-up charge, and while Mrs Hollis had worked in the laundry, she'd been tarred by the accusations. Albert could only thank his mother again for her care of the Hollis family.

"Your mother looked after us. She had us sent to the manor, which is a fine place. You haven't yet visited, have you?"

Albert shook his head as deep emotions swam close to the surface.

"When you go, your mother's portrait is in the gallery. Lovely, truly showed her heart. She'd be so pleased if she could see you now. So happy, with a fine woman and those two sweet little girls. And speaking of them, I have a grandson now. He's so clever!"

"He is. Fred will teach him to ride and all the things he'll need to know in Australia."

"Is it... Is it as big as Fred says? He says it will take near a week to reach his house. And he told me I'm to have a small house of my own, if that's what I want, and Laura can take up sewing, be a seamstress. Is it really that simple?"

Clearing his throat, Albert leaned in. "He's said if you don't like the property, he'll purchase a house for you in Brisbane, the major city in the north. All you must do is tell him what you want."

Mrs Hollis gaped. "But... Can he afford that? I mean, he's only a farmer!"

Albert laughed, then realised that she was thinking along the lines of one of the tenants. Tenant farmers were not capable of supporting a second family; they usually were reliant on their landlord to ensure their livelihood. It reinforced to him that he'd need to split his time between the two countries, ensuring they were well cared for, and the needs of his tenants was a vital component of his new, long-term plan.

"He's done very well for himself," Albert assured Mrs Hollis. "He owns the property free and clear, and we're both making a good living." As the breakfast broke up, he stood and cleared his throat. "Mrs Hollis and Laura, it will be some time before I see you again, as I have business this morning, but I wish you fair seas and safe travels." He looked to Louisa. "Will you ride with me this morning?"

She blinked. "I should stay here. Mrs Hollis and—"

"Oh no, dear. You have commitments, and I will be leaving as soon as my Fred can arrange seats on the mail."

"You aren't travelling by mail coach, Mrs Hollis. I've arranged a coachman to take you direct to London in my travelling carriage," Albert explained.

"Oh, but..."

"No buts. It's done, and all we need to do is await its arrival," Fred answered. "We aren't poor anymore, Mama. I can afford this, and what's more, you'll be taking a purse with you to pay for incidentals. You've a hotel already booked, and your fare all the way to Moreton Bay is covered. I gave Laura the packet with the tickets yesterday and the coin too."

Mrs Hollis stared, then burst into tears. Amelia was up and swept around to the woman, enveloping her. "He's more than able, Mrs Hollis, and this family," she said, sweeping her gaze across the entire room, "this family cares for its own."

It took long minutes for the emotions to settle in the room, and while Albert may have felt a touch impatient, he knew the ups and downs of their situation were finally being smoothed out, so he waited until Louisa smiled at him and nodded from the other end of the table.

"Will you ride?" he asked as she rose and stepped around to join him.

"Yes, then, I shall. I just need time to change."

"Go," he urged. "But no more than half an hour."

"Sooner if I can," she answered then left the room.

❧

Dusk was setting in as they returned to the house. The rounds had taken much longer than planned, but Louisa now knew the true state of affairs. Just how much effort Albert and his people had already put in, and how much more was necessary.

"When do you think we'll be in a position to leave?" she queried as they walked their horses companionably toward the house.

"It will be months yet, but I'm thinking, with us having things begun here, we could take the girls to the Manor. I don't recall ever going there, my grandparents were old when Mama married my father. They passed when I was quite young, and—" He stopped his horse. "Louisa," he murmured. He didn't know why, but something urged him to pause and wait. To stop her horse too.

She did and looked at him. "What?"

"I don't know. A feeling," he murmured.

A crash sounded, quite nearby, and he turned to seek the cause of the sound. Her horse gave a wild whinny as it reared in fright, then dashed off, with Louisa hanging on to the reins.

He kicked the side of his mount, terror building inside him. He'd seen horses react like this, to the fright. In his experience, unless the rider was exceptionally skilled, it ended badly.

I won't lose her. Not now, when I've just found paradise.

He leaned low, chasing after the horse which galloped through the wooded areas in front of him, while Louisa's hat trailed behind her, held only by a silly scarf. It might snag on a tree limb and tug her off, or even worse...

Albert urged his horse to move faster. He was gaining when Louisa suddenly hauled again on the reins and her horse started to slow enough that he could come alongside her. "Let go," he instructed, and she did as his arm snaked around her and pulled her over. For an instant she dangled until he pulled her into his lap.

Her arms twisted around him, tight and strong, and he thanked

God he was able to pull her safely into his arms as his mount slowed, then stopped.

Her chest bellowed, and he realised she was crying silently, huddled into his embrace. "I was so frightened. I don't know what happened..."

Unable to speak, he simply held her and soaked in the knowledge that she was safe and well, in his arms. When he could finally lift his eyes, it was to see the outline of her horse, now stopped a long distance from them. For an instant he considered leaving it, but his mind reminded him he couldn't. No responsible owner would leave their horse unattended, so he walked his over. Once he'd gathered the reins, he tied them to his pommel, and they turned for home.

"Did anything happen specifically before she spooked?" Albert asked.

Louisa shrugged. "Not that I could discern, just she took fright and was bolting before I could stop it."

He grunted and kept his horse calm while they walked toward the stables. He kept alert though, lest anything happen again, but it didn't. When the stableman took his horse, he dismounted then assisted Louisa to do the same. Albert released her hand and stepped up to the horse in time to note a small rivulet of blood dripping from a shallow graze on the mount's hind quarter. "What's this?" he wondered aloud.

"Someone 'as tried to shoot it, I'd say," the man answered, crowding in. "See as 'ow it's a line? I'd say someone either 'as a bad aim or..." He didn't finish, merely shook his head and took the reins. "I'll clean it up and apply some salve. She'll be sore and steady for a few days, I reckon." He led the horse into the stable, leaving the two of them in silence.

Albert's lips thinned, and he wondered if it was more that someone had somehow found out about the information he'd received from Corvings just this morning? The information about Louisa's problem.

Lost in thought, he never heard the footsteps and was unaware of someone else being present until the person cleared their throat.

"So, thought you'd wriggle out of it, did you, Louisa? Thought you could get rid of me that easily?" Albert looked up to see a wild woman, dressed in black, her hair flying in the slight breeze, and a crazed look in her eye. In her hand, waved a gun. Was this Pamela Jezerey? The woman who'd been making Louisa's life hell for so long?

"Pamela Jezerey," breathed Louisa. "Why have you come here?"

He heard the frustration and anger in her tone and hoped she'd hold onto her temper. He needed to think of a way to get them both out of this mess, without the woman shooting either of them.

"You messed up my life," the woman groused. "Asked questions that I shouldn't have to answer. My husband..." She stamped her feet. "He's furious with me. Said he'll cast me off unless I sort this out." Her eyes glinted, and Albert detected a hint of madness in their depths.

"I never—"

"Shut up!" the woman screamed at Louisa, and his wife, heaven bless her, stilled and closed her mouth.

"I made the enquiries," he stated, wanting to change Pamela's attention to him. If he could just get Louisa out of there, they might have a hope.

"You? An idiot farm boy with more money than sense? The spare who made good?" Pamela's voice dripped with hatred, while the gun bobbed in her hand.

"Yes, me. The Earl of Conney."

Now the woman laughed, discordant and loud, and Albert willed Louisa to understand, to begin to slide away, toward the stables and safety, but she didn't.

"You've been attempting to blackmail me, Pamela. But the child isn't my responsibility. If Jeremy was the father, that is separate to me." Louisa spoke forcefully, and the woman turned, lifted the gun once more, and Albert wanted to scream.

"I made enquiries," Albert said. "My man of business, he asked the questions, and the child isn't Jeremy's, is it? You and your husband cooked up the scheme, because your funds are low. Jeremy wasn't the only one you duped."

"Shut up," Pamela bellowed, her hands wavering. "I talk, you listen, then you pay. You pay lots. *You fix this*!" Her voice rose with every word, until in the end it was shrill.

Perhaps if he could keep her talking, others would hear and come. Assist him in overpowering the woman who was vibrating before him.

Louisa made to move, and Albert flung out his hand. "Stay still," he instructed in a low murmur.

"What are you saying?" Pamela demanded.

"Just that my wife stays here. I can pay," he answered, needing to draw her closer to the house. Out into the open.

"No. She pays. *She ruined my life*!" Spittle flew, and Albert knew then that the only way out was to lunge. But would he be fast enough?

"I never ruined your life, Pamela." Louisa shook. "I was an innocent victim. I didn't take anything away from you."

"Innocent? That's rich. You had it all. A husband, money, and a family that's loaded. I just wanted my share. I carried that bastard for nine months in my belly. I told Jeremy it was his, and when the brat was born, he celebrated. Did he tell you that? Did he tell you about the diamond bracelet he gave me for bearing him a child?" Each word was designed to wound Louisa, and rage burned in Albert, but he had to think past it all. Needed to be calm and weigh the danger up.

From the corner of his eye, he saw a face, then another, as Fred and the stableman waited in the shadows. He just needed Pamela to focus for another few minutes, to get her to focus on him. To draw her away.

"Your husband knew all along, didn't he?" Albert said. "You both cooked this up, to what? Shore up his sagging finances? To give you something to live on? The child though, no one has seen it for some time."

Pamela turned, her face caught in a sneering visage. "It's served its purpose. I cast it off and sent it to the orphanage." She cackled and Louisa gasped.

Before the woman could turn again, Albert lunged, his hand reaching for the wavering pistol.

A sound echoed. Loud.

Heat seared his side, but he grabbed her hand.

She jerked and tried to pull away.

Voices came then, yelling. Demanding she drop the gun.

An arm wound around him as he lurched, the pain in his side ballooning.

Grey edged his vision and he dropped to the ground.

Albert fell, and Louisa launched forward, fearing the worst. Blood seeped, and she cried out, "Albert!"

Pamela laughed wildly, the sound discordant. "I ruined your life!"

Louisa whirled in time to see the woman lunge at her, even though the men had reached out and grabbed Pamela's arms.

"Let me go, you filthy creature," Pamela screamed at Louisa.

Fury bloomed inside Louisa's chest. The small pistol had fallen to the ground in the scuffle, and for an instant, the thought of revenge inched into Louisa's mind, then melted away. That wouldn't help Albert, and right now he was her concern.

"Get the doctor," Louisa yelled.

She stripped off her jacket, the movements jerky and instinctive. Dropping to the ground, she heard Albert's groan, but he wasn't truly conscious, and for that she was grateful as she shoved the balled-up material against him.

"Take her into custody," she muttered, not needing the added problem of dealing with the mad woman, who continued to scream at them.

The stablemaster came out with ropes and they restrained the woman, then dragged her away, while footmen rushed out of the house and lifted the injured Earl and carried him inside.

Even as she followed, Louisa called instructions, "Call the doctor. I'll need clean warm water and bandages. Hurry!"

***

Louisa paced the hallway, waiting for the doctor to finish with his patient. Albert had bled copiously, and it was sheer luck the physician had been visiting a woman in labour on the estate and was able to attend immediately.

Her brain ached, the headache teaming up with the queasiness of her stomach. Blood, scarlet and running down his side, had urged her forward. She'd acted instinctively, tugging off her jacket and wadding it up before applying it against the wound.

She barely remembered screaming for help, only that her entire focus had been Albert in those long moments.

The door opened and the portly doctor emerged, tugging his glasses from his face. "Madam, I've had the chance to examine the Earl. He's lucky. The bullet went straight through, but as with all these wounds, the greatest danger now is infection."

"The blood?"

"There was a lot, I agree, but he's a strong man. So long as we keep a watch on the wound, and it doesn't turn septic, he'll make a full recovery."

Louisa clenched her hands together. "So?"

"You'll need someone to stay with him at all times, the wound must be kept clean, and he mustn't be allowed to move. I've stitched him up, but should he take the fever, then..." He shrugged.

The words were stones which filled her belly. "He won't be alone at all. The maids and I will take turns."

"Very well then. I must return to Mrs Jones. Should you need me, send for me and I'll come. If he does take the fever, I need to know."

He glanced at her. "You're looking pale, and that won't help him." Then he nodded and trotted off, his bag in one hand and glasses in the other.

Elspeth and Isabelle rose from the seats by Albert's door. "Dearest, we'll help," they offered, but Louisa shook her head.

"No. Not right now. I need..." She glanced at the door, then looked back to her sisters. "I'm going in to check on Albert. Can you please handle the household for now? Mrs Coombs and I will take control of his needs. The girls will need to be settled and..." She shrugged. "I need Albert," she muttered and headed for the room. Her hand settled on the knob, and she turned. "Thank you," she whispered then entered the room.

***

Albert didn't know what was happening or where he was. A voice echoed, telling him that he would be fine, but he needed to wake up. He knew the sound of the voice. He knew the woman. The voice called to his inner self, but his body couldn't yet make the connection, because the pressure on his eyes made it impossible to open them. The darkness tugged him under once more.

Heat filled him, torching him, like a spit-roast.

"Come back to me, Albert. Please? I need you." The voice in his brain urged him to wake, to cast off the layers of whatever held him under. There was despair in the tone, but it still wasn't enough. He couldn't make his eyes open, or his brain comprehend why she was so upset. All he knew was he needed to be where she was. Why couldn't he?

His mouth opened, but the words didn't emerge, and besides, what was it he meant to say? Reality spun away once again.

Three days had passed. Louisa shifted in the seat where she'd hunched beside Albert in the bed. He'd taken a fever on the second day. The doctor had visited and tutted, hovering beside the bed. He even patted her hand and insisted that with care Albert would pull through.

Another long day passed, with her waiting by his side. Praying and hopeful.

Now the house rested. She'd sent Mrs Coombs to bed several hours ago, leaving Louisa to care for her husband.

Sleep called like a siren, and she groaned, turned in the chair, and the blanket dropped to the floor. As she bent to retrieve it, a sound emanated from Albert's mouth. Not quite a groan, but... "Lo...ui...sa?"

She sat back upright. "Albert?"

He groaned, "Lou... Louisa? Where am I?"

Tears filled her eyes. "Oh Albert! You're awake! I'm so happy." She gripped his hands tight.

"What happened?"

His words were thick, and she instinctively reached for the invalid cup Mrs Coombs had found for her. It looked like a teapot, with a spout but no top.

Albert sipped and Louisa waited. She wouldn't rush him. Not now. He'd had a rough few days and would need to regain his strength.

"Louisa? Pamela. Where is she?" He shifted on the bed and groaned, while Louisa winced in sympathy.

Louisa slid the cup to the table, took his hand. "The men took her into custody, and she's been transferred, but it's doubtful she'll be able to face court. The doctor said he believes she's suffering from a type of hysterical madness. He's making representations that she should be sent to an asylum where she can be cared for. The magistrate has indicated he feels that's appropriate."

Albert licked his lips, and once again, Louisa picked up the cup, waiting patiently as he sipped. "Her husband?" he asked.

Louisa sighed. "He's been sent for, but I think the truth is, he's happy she's in the place best suited to her needs. As for the child..." Louisa swiped at her cheeks. "She died two years ago, in a fall. It seems that is likely the reason Pamela lost her grip on reality, according to the doctor."

"So, you're free of Pamela."

"It would seem so, but there's so much pain involved. So many losses, and it all stems from two people choosing to dismiss the needs of those who most cared for them." But Louisa couldn't find it in her heart to be angry. Albert was alive and would recover.

"You're unhurt?"

She nodded. "The only one hurt was you. I thought you'd die," she whispered. "The doctor stitched up your wound, but the temperature you had... I didn't know if you'd make it." She refused to brush away the tears that rose. Deep inside her, the need to let him see how much he mattered to her welled. "I don't want to lose you, Albert. We've just begun, and I couldn't believe that you'd be stolen from me. Not now, at the beginning."

His hand reached out and she took it. Gripped him tight and noted that while his might be weak, he seemed a little brighter as they spoke. "I'm not going anywhere, except where you are, my Louisa."

"You should rest," she urged.

"Only if you're beside me."

She laughed because he was as weak as a newborn kitten but demanding her presence. She climbed onto the bed, resting on top of the sheets, because she refused to run the risk of bumping him.

"Just for a moment," she muttered and laid her head on the shoulder away from his injured side. "In the morning, we'll get you up and bathed. Change the bedding."

"Thank you," he whispered as his eyes closed. "Thank you for loving me and caring."

EPILOGUE

Albert hated the waiting, the pacing. In the room beyond, he heard Louisa crying out. Every ounce of his being demanded he should be in there with her.

No one would let him in. Instead, he waited and fretted.

Finally, the sound he longed for, the cry of a newborn, split the air. Surging up out of his chair, he hurried to the door, which opened.

The doctor hovered. "Sir, they're just now cleaning up your wife, then you may enter. Your children are both here and well."

Impatience bit at him. "And?"

"A daughter. A son. Both of good size." The doctor slid his glasses from his nose and wiped them on a cloth he'd dragged from his pockets. "Your wife came through very well, I suppose two previous deliveries likely assisted, but she'll need to rest. Foods should be easily digestible, and excitation limited."

"When can I see her? And the babies?" His heart raced at the thought of a new daughter and a son. *Three daughters and a son. Indeed, I've been rewarded.*

The door opened and two nursemaids filled the corridor of the house. Twin swaddled bundles took up his vision. "My daughter and son?"

Mrs Coombs nodded. "Aye. The countess will be ready to see you soon, and we'll send for Miss Eleanora and Miss Marina."

"No excitation, as I'm sure I've already explained," the doctor said.

Mrs Coombs smiled, the lines of her face smoothing out. "Indeed, but the two misses will be quiet, I'm sure. "

Albert knew the smile, the sly wink she gifted him reinforcing what he knew.

The door opened a third time and the nurse he'd hired for Louisa in the closing days of her pregnancy hovered. "Your Grace? If you'd like to visit with your wife?"

Ignoring all else, he pushed his way to the door. Bright sunlight filled the room, and Louisa lay in the large bed, pale but awake and sitting up. "Albert? The babies?"

He beckoned the women and the babies to join him in the room. A bassinette had been set up beside Louisa's bed, and the ladies carefully laid their precious cargo within it, then left the room, so there were just the four of them.

"Here's our new daughter and our son." Albert wasn't sure he was game to pick either up; he sweated just at the thought.

"A son. A daughter," breathed Louisa, her smile wreathing her face. "You have an heir."

"Even better, we have a family, Louisa. One we'll make together, and spend long, happy days with." He took the spot on the side of the bed and grasped her hand. "The family you gave me."

She tugged her hand from his, then cupped his cheek. "The one we made together. Now then — "

He shook his head, stopping her words. "I think Mrs Coombs is having the girls brought down, so they can meet their brother and sister."

In the year since he'd married Louisa, both the girls had begun calling him Papa, and he loved that. He adored the two girls, and he'd discovered that family time could be a joy.

The last of the shadows on his heart, the ones his father and brother had painted there, had finally melted away. Soon, as a family, they would set sail for Australia. Louisa's pregnancy and the risk of twins kept them longer than he'd planned. Now he could return to their other home, taking his wife and children to settle on their property, which abutted with Frederick's, along with Amelia and their family, who'd gone ahead of them so many months before.

Life had granted him treasures above rubies, and contentment filled Albert as he looked at his wife. "I love you."

She grinned. "I love you too."

The knocking at the door indicated the rest of their immediate family had arrived.

The End

Did you enjoy this book by Imogene Nix?
There's more on the following pages. Just keep turning to see what else.

THE CELTIC CUPID TRILOGY

When Cupid—otherwise known as Diocail— is banished from his home on a remote Scottish Island, he's set a series of tasks by the great god Lugh, who also happens to be his father.

In **Blame The Wine**, he must bring two lovers together... BBW Cara and James, the man she's lusted over from afar who happens to be a super geek and head Veha Industries.

In **A Stranger's Embrace**, Diocail is driven to help an emotionally fragile Jane and Davis, a famous author. The task is more complicated, with the existence of Carstairs her could-be ex-husband and teenage daughter, Frannie.

In **Revenge on Cupid**, Diocail must take the ultimate chance and find his own happily ever after with Simone. Sometimes the past gets in the way and HEA's don't come cheap though.

The dusty, dingy little diner was full, even with its current state of cleanliness—or lack thereof. People from the surrounding offices didn't care about anything except the incredible, well-prepared food at a reasonable cost. They flooded in, like waves to the shore. As one tide left, another swept in.

"Honestly, Simone. I'm going to try getting his attention one more time. If that doesn't work, I'm out of there. I mean, how long can I keep trying?" Cara picked at the caramel tart she hadn't been able to resist with the cheap metal fork and flicked the blob of fresh cream that sat on top to the side of the plate.

"You've said that tons of times before. Besides, what are you going to do to get his attention? Hmm? Walk naked through the typing pool?" Simone bobbed the straw in her smoothie as she eyed her friend with a frown. "It's been what? Eighteen months since you saw him, and you've mooned over him from a distance ever since you met him. You need to move on, Cara. That is, unless there's something you haven't shared?"

The query was arch. Cara shivered even as she shook her head. "No."

Simone quirked an eyebrow, obviously unconvinced with the answer. Cara let out a deep sigh of frustration. "There's a position...it's only temporary, for a PA reporting directly to him." She speared a forkful of tart, chewed quickly and swallowed, before continuing. "In his office, full-time for the period of the engagement. I saw the memo yesterday. I mean, I have the skills, right? I can type, answer phones, make coffee, file, greet people. What's more, I can probably do it better than all those size eights in the typing pool that

Ms. Jackman seems to prefer." She nodded thoughtfully. "All I have to do is get past the ogre in Human Resources."

Simone stared at her, disbelief clear on her face. "Girl, I so remember that woman. If you think you can get past her, you're doing better than I ever did. That's why I left Veha Industries, remember? Maybe it's time to haul out your resumé and consider some other options. Look for something better." Simone shook her head and billows of her crimson hair swirled through the still air.

Cara understood Simone only had her best interests at heart. But this time she knew the outcome would be different. Hell, she could feel it in the air. The tingle of expectation.

"Cara, the HR ogre will hang you out for breakfast before she offers you anything like a position in that office. Remember her mantra? Good looks and good work make for a positive workplace!"

Simone didn't sugar-coat anything. It was another great reason for their long- term friendship. Honesty. But Cara didn't want to hear the truth in the statement. Even if it was exactly as her friend said.

Cara nodded quickly. "Yeah, I know, but if I don't try, then I won't know how close I can get to him, right? And the only way to catch his attention is to get past *her* and see him in person." Cara quaked a little at the information she needed to share. The favor she needed to ask. "Anyway, I tidied up my resumé and dropped the application into a memo envelope yesterday, so it's too late to back out now. I mean, fortune favors the brave. Doesn't it? If I don't snag an interview, I'm going to visit the career advisor across the street and register with them." She shrugged. "I'll look for temp work until something more long-term shows up. I can see what they have on offer and well...who knows? Maybe a job with the right boss is just waiting for me. But I'd rather this worked out, to be honest." Her voice trailed off into a whisper. "I really wish he would notice me."

Simone took a long slurp of her banana drink, and Cara noticed her questioning gaze even as she squirmed. Finally, Simone nodded. "It's your funeral. So anyway, you'd better show me this memo if you want me to be a referee for you. I'm guessing that's what you need, right? I'll have to know what I'm supposed to say about you before they ring."

Cara smiled. "Thanks, Simone. I knew I could count on you." She slipped a piece of paper out of her handbag and handed it over. "Sorry it's a bit creased. It was in the bottom of my bag, I stashed it so none of the others from the pool would see. You know how it is."

Available from Love Books Publishing
books2read.com/CelticCupid

Direct Autographed Copy
https://www.imogenenix.net/CelticCupid

STAR OF ISHTAR

Warriors of the Elector
Book One

The first time Elara laid eyes on Grayson was when he rescued her from the clutches of a madman and his scientists who were kidnapping humans and conducting horrific experiments on them. That was years ago. In spite of her attempts to deepen their relationship, they remained nothing more than close friends.Now Elara is a medic with the Admiralty, and she knows what she wants. It's been Grayson since the beginning. When Elara is stationed on the *Star of Ishtar*, she arrives with a plan to further her career. But this time her plan has an added bonus—to finally get her man.

Grayson's spent years fighting the connection between himself and Elara. He's certain it only exist because he saved her life. But his will is failing, and he fears he just might give in to temptation.

"I finally made it." Elara Sudonne watched as the hull of the *Star of Ishtar* loomed in the inky darkness. She clutched her hands tightly together as the shuttle approached the hulking battleship.

This would be her new home and first combat ST placement for the Earth Empire. She quaked inwardly with nerves but fought to keep her serene exterior. Previously her deployments had consisted solely of on-planet expeditions and in rehabilitation and dirtside facilities. When the chance had arisen to move to the battleship, she'd grabbed it with both hands.

The frigid air chilled her bones as she sat in her shuttle seat, but a trickle of sweat inched its way down her back under the fresh gray wool flight uniform. Little puffs of vapor escaped her mouth as she rubbed her arms. Nerves stretched tight, she looked through the small portal at the front of the vessel. She wanted to tug at the collar that somehow seemed to have grown tighter as the ship loomed ahead, but instead she firmed her mouth, straightened her spine, and concentrated on the future.

"So damned long." She'd been working toward this outcome since the day Grayson Myatt and Duvall McCord had saved her from her Ru'Edan captors. She was lucky, she'd survived the 'experimentation' of the Ru'Edan leader Crick Sur Banden's scientists. "And all I have to remind me are my scars." She didn't grin at her own joke.

The person seated behind her jostled but she ignored it, lost in her memories. On that day, so very long ago, the young Elara, fresh-faced and with idealistic views of the empire, was taken from the mall where she'd been shopping with friends, thrust into the back of a transport vehicle, and given to the Ru'Edan scientists to experiment on.

For days they'd worked on her and others, seeking an average pain threshold of humans, slicing her skin then noting reactions and how long it took to heal. They'd cut her arms, body, and even her face, and now she carried the extensive scarring of the exercise as a reminder to herself and others of what they were fighting for. Freedom. The freedom of Earth and its allied planets.

She'd never relinquished hope, it had been her constant companion as she fought against the all-consuming terror. Then they'd found her in that dirty, disused warehouse. They'd found others too, in various states of death and decay. The smells of despair had filled the air with a fetid ripeness that she'd never been able to forget.

Since that day she'd promised herself that she would pay the Ru'Edan back for what they'd done to her. What they'd taken from her. Over the years, she tempered and honed the rage while remaining adamant that she would see the final act played out. She couldn't physically fight, but she had learned about trauma, knew it and understood how it affected a person, and used it as a weapon.

The iron will forged through her experiences had fed her determination, and she'd applied herself to study, finishing in the top ten percent of her class. She entered the medical program at the academy, working hard to excel. Her family remained supportive if perplexed as to why she had chosen to keep reminding herself of what had happened.

The maw of the *Star of Ishtar* loomed closer, opening its cavernous mouth as she watched through the portal. She could hear the voices of the shuttle crew signaling their intention to enter and land, the tinny confirmation coming swiftly. She watched avidly while the shuttle maneuvered, imagining the invisible shields dropping to allow it entry.

Her hands twisted with fear and anger, but she tamped down her emotions. Anger never helped anyone. Staying strong, knowing your history, and ensuring it couldn't be repeated, they were the answers, she told herself firmly, pulling herself from the grip of a dark past so horrific she still saw it in her dreams. She pushed it away to the recesses of her mind and focused on what she was about to do.

A squark overhead, the usual mechanical sound that alerted all on board to a transmission by the captain, caught her attention. "Attention all passengers. We are entering the shuttle bay. Please ensure when you disembark you remove all personal items. Move beyond the white line and wait for your designation."

The lights of the bay flashed as they entered, and once again Elara marveled at how far humanity had moved since they had first walked the Earth. She saw the opening of the structure as the shuttle moved into the bay, inching forward slowly until it stopped its ponderous motion and began its descent to the floor. Something deep inside warmed even as the shuttle's environmental systems began to synchronize with the cooler temperature of the *Star of Ishtar*, and she felt a smile crawl its way over her face.

Elara breathed in deeply, inhaling the metallic-tasting, recycled air and welcoming the calmness that settled on her body. Her eyes closed as she filled her lungs. "I'm here." There was more than a little satisfaction in her tone, and she smiled. She slowly exhaled, finding that center of peace she relied on.

A loud thud and clank echoed as the deep drone split the air. The engines were powering down, and there she was, on one of the Earth Empire's Emeritus class battleships. She sat in her seat, waiting for the all clear from the captain, and once it sounded through the cabin, she rose, tugging at the webbing belt and disengaging it.

The small backpack beside her was all she carried as she made her way to the exit, not needing to duck as so many others did. She stepped through the door, her hands gripping the rail of the cold, metal stairs which connected to the side of the gray shuttle.

She clambered down them slowly, savoring the experience. The sting of the cold on her hands from the stairs, frigid from even their brief exposure to the blackness of space, made her flinch inwardly. The shuttle journey from the Admiralty's strategic base at Aenna to their current position had taken just over an hour, but the whole time it felt like her heart had been in her throat. Her mouth was dry as she followed the new recruits from the ship into the landing bay. She stopped, silently noting the slight mustiness of the air, the recycled quality easily recognizable. Everything, including the oxygen, needed recycling in space.

All around her people swarmed, either around the ships or into the dogleg line that now formed ahead of her. Someone had opened the baggage locker of the shuttle, and the sound of dropping bags hitting the plascrete floor echoed in the air. Another crewmember guided trolleys to the other side of the shuttle, pulling out boxes with important day-to-day items for the ship, including vaccines and plants. She watched briefly, all the while listening to the alien cacophony. Voices called in welcome to old crewmembers, while new ones watched, many goggle-eyed in the fresh uniforms of newly minted officers and crewmembers.

Her gaze flicked around quickly, taking in the sights, sounds, and smells, pungent with oils and grease; burning smells from the scorched plascrete and the press of sweaty or nervous bodies. She joined the line silently, tacking onto the end, and stayed at parade rest, knowing the welcoming voice would cut through the air soon enough. She felt somehow disconnected from the main throng. Perhaps the knowledge that this was the outcome she had worked for years to achieve set her apart. However, still, she felt so...distant from everything around her. She smiled secretly at the bout of whimsy.

"Attention!" The voice boomed out over the plascrete of the docking bay, and she snapped her body into position, noting the commander who had bellowed the words. Technically, she outranked most members aboard the *Star of Ishtar*, except for the command and leadership staff, but she knew all newcomers had to join the welcoming parade, regardless of rank.

Fleet Captain Elphin came into view, his tired features topped by salt-and-pepper gray hair, which highlighted his cool blue eyes. Elara also recognized a body prone to a little middle-aged thickness. Following behind him was his second-in-command, Duvall McCord. A young up-and-coming officer, his status as a fast-tracking officer heading toward his own command, with Elphin both his mentor and captain, had become almost legendary at the academy.

She looked closely at McCord, noting the dynamic drive of his actions and movements. Soon he would achieve a promotion to captain, and she rejoiced for her friend. She'd followed his career with interest and had to tamp down a smile as his eyes betrayed the shock of seeing her before settling into their flat command persona. So he hadn't been apprised of her deployment, she noted, and she had to restrain the tiny feeling of surprise and satisfaction. She filed that snippet of information away.

She caught sight of the man standing behind Duvall. Grayson Myatt. He'd made her heart beat faster for years. Tall and blond with a muscular build and a sexy, tight, little butt, he had pools of deep-blue eyes that had always made her think of forever. He had a growth of stubble on his chiseled jaw, and her fingers itched to touch his perfect lips. Yes, since the day he'd found her in that nasty ware-house tied down like a ragged animal, she'd worshipped him from afar.

Now she had her opportunity to tangle with him, hopefully much closer than any chance that had ever come her way before. With a sigh, she pulled her gaze back to the captain and forced herself to concentrate on his words. She couldn't afford to have her commanding officer angry due to her being distracted.

"Welcome to the *Star of Ishtar*. Most academy recruits want to join us because of what we represent, but on this ship, we only take the best of the best. So, if you made it here, you're the ones we wanted to take a look at. Getting here is only the first step. Staying here is harder to achieve. Our people are the best. Earn your place, and in return, we'll make you one of our crew—a member of the *Star of Ishtar*. Only the best and the brightest wear our uniform and badge. You'll be expected to perform to your absolute limit then give some more. We don't tolerate people who don't pull their weight. Do us proud and wear your uniform with pride." The captain looked out over the new members of his crew. His voice had echoed during his speech, and now it died away.

He scanned the faces before him, and she could almost read his thoughts. There were new security officers and a smattering of other crew. Some of them were young and impressionable, and she knew a few wouldn't make the cut as crewmembers. Others would carve out their place on the *Star of Ishtar* and move to better positions and placements, like she would: the new SurgiTech, a younger female, experienced but untried on board a ship. She smiled at that thought.

Some of those who stood with her would be replaced as they failed the exacting standards the captain set. She'd heard that he was a firm captain, fair but demanding. He'd have to be to command this ship. The Ishtar had well over five hundred at full capacity, and the captain could select their placements as his command staff saw fit from the many who applied to join the crew. She sensed his satisfaction with the choices in the relaxation of his body.

Abruptly, he turned to Duvall, breaking her study of him. "Get them to where they need to present themselves." His words echoed as he walked away. He had a purposeful stride. Quick but unhurried, like he knew where he was going and how to get there. A man who knew how to get what he wanted. Someone to respect and admire.

"My name is Commander Duvall McCord. I am your second-in-command, and my direct subordinate is Commander Grayson Myatt. While you are aboard the *Star of Ishtar* you will be required to fulfill your duties efficiently. As Captain Elphin said, do your job right and you will be one of ours, with all the benefits that come with being a crewmember of the *Star of Ishtar*."

He paused and eyeballed each of the newer recruits, those fresh from the academy. Many of them paled under his gaze, and she smiled inwardly. Even the older people in the line seemed to quake beneath his scowl. He'd always had that air of innate authority, even when barely out of the academy himself. She knew his methods and watched him make full use of the carefully practiced tone of presence.

"Each of you has been assigned. You will present yourselves to the chief of your section. Those details will be found in your orders. Commander Myatt has organized a team to escort you to your cabins. You will have approximately one hour to prepare. We've arranged for crewmembers to escort you to your superiors. Be ready to present for duty. Any issues, you will, of course, take up with your section commander. Should there be need to take any further action, you will see Commander Myatt. You should only see me if you are a command crewmember or as a point of discipline. I am not one for small talk, so if you present to me, have a very good reason."

He delivered the words slowly and deliberately, and Elara restrained a small smile on hearing at least one gulp from those in the line nearest her.

"We run a tight ship here. Discipline and commitment are the two key factors we look for beyond loyalty in our crew. You will from henceforth represent our ship everywhere, and we do not tolerate anything less than the best." He looked around once more, the stern demeanor he wore so well reinforcing the message. If she hadn't known him for so long, she too might have missed the hint of humor glinting in his eyes, the one many took for coldness.

Her legs ached, and she wanted to move and relieve the pressure on them, but she held herself still, waiting for the command to dismiss. She wouldn't let herself or him down now. Not after she'd worked so long to achieve this position.

As the new ST, she had no previous experience on ships. She had vast experience in the field, but Elara was aware that would count for little in the eyes of most of the crew. She didn't intend to signal a weakness to anyone and least of all on her first day aboard the *Star of Ishtar*. That thought held her still and controlled.

She had big shoes to fill after her predecessor, Jamieson, had retired, even though she knew she could fill the void he'd left behind. As a long-term member of the crew—over twenty years—his tenure on the *Star of Ishtar* had placed him aboard since its launch. Due to his experience in the heat of battle with the Ru'Edan he had made a name for himself as the coldest of cold in the hottest of situations. She hoped to emulate that herself and carve out her own place aboard the Ishtar, as its crew lovingly knew her.

Duvall and Grayson knew how much she wanted to prove herself. They just wouldn't have expected it here, on the Ishtar.

She watched Duvall study her, then, quickly turning on his heel, call to those assembled, "Dismissed."

Once they started to move away, she softened her stance, preparing to turn when the call came.

"Sudonne! A moment if you please."

Elara turned to face Duvall. "Commander?"

"Welcome to the *Star of Ishtar*, Elara. While I am surprised you're the new ST, Grayson and I are pleased you could join us. But how did you manage to pull it off? Keeping it quiet that you were the new ST?" he asked, his voice deep enough to make most women shiver with anticipation.

She smiled, thinking it was a shame she didn't have any feelings for him except sisterly attachment, but then again, given his lack of deep commitment to women, maybe it wasn't such a shame after all.

She understood what drove him. He wanted his own ship and to captain his own future. They'd spent many nights over wine or ale discussing his beliefs that commitment grounded a person. Inwardly, she shrugged. He'd make those calls for himself, though she was sure that one day he would come across someone who would make him consider his choices a little more thoroughly.

"I'm pleased to be here, Duvall. Having an uncle who happens to be an admiral, he was able to let Captain Elphin know that I wanted to surprise you. It's a small world in the Admiralty. Elphin already knew of me, so he okayed my placement. Once the powers knew there was no impediments to me joining the crew, it was fairly simple from there." She felt a small smile creep onto her face, then let it drop away. "What do you think Grayson thinks?"

"Ah, still chasing him, are you?" He grinned, his eyes twinkling. "I think he'll be pleased you're finally old enough and you're here." He looked her straight in the eye. "But you may just need to remind him of that particular fact." He motioned for her to go before him, barking out a deep laugh. "Come on, I'll show you to your cabin."

Available from Love Books Publishing
Available in Ebook via Books2Read

Direct Autographed Copy
https://www.imogenenix.net/Warriors1

THE BLOOD BRIDE BY IMOGENE NIX

Hope just wants to be an ordinary nestling. She went to college and escaped, but now she's back and there's a secret everyone is keeping from her.

Xavier is the new master of the nest, ready to welcome home the daughter of the house who he has never met. He's unprepared for the woman who steals his breath and enchants him.

Now Hope and Xavier must fight for lives and those of the innocents. After all, it is only by overcoming the rogues that they will have a chance of a timeless future together. But will it be in time?

❧

PROLOGUE

As silence descended on the house, the shadows grew—dark grays and blacks that bled into each other. First one figure then another broke away, making a run toward the house. Silent as the grave, they moved swiftly over dew-slicked grass. Then they stopped still. Waiting. Not a movement betrayed them until a signal propelled them back into action and they started crawling upwards. The walls damp coating no barrier to the intruders that ascended in the darkness.

The sound of each window breaking shattered the quiet—the figures were inside. Screams echoed through the night. Yet, in this area of large estates, heavy with noise-absorbing shrubbery, no one could hear those within. The blood-curdling screams went on and on before finally dying away.

Just one sound echoed through the night: The sobbing of a child.

The front door opened and figures trooped out—ghostly specters against an inky night sky, broken by a single outline. A child in white, carried at the center of the pack.

No sound broke the silence as they moved toward the trees surrounded the house.

Flames now licked at the manor: A deathly glow of oily smoke rising.

All that remained was a single person—wrapped in a cape of midnight blue beyond the house—watching them melt away.

Jemima moved toward the burning structure, breaking into a run as she breached the threshold. Vainly she attempted to enter, but the heat drove her back.

Now dashing tears from her face, she raced across the graveled driveway toward the gates, where the guardhouse was located. No sign of life existed within the building and some instinct of survival slowed her pace to a careful creep. Out of breath and heaving from exertion, she nervously checked within.

Small puffs of white vapor colored the glass. She darted from one window to another. Her cloak drawn tightly around her body, hoping it would camouflage her from sight.

Satisfied, Jemima entered through the heavy, wooden front door and moved toward the phone she spied on the floor. Her eyes darting here and there she dialed, listening to the rotary motor as it returned to the proper position. Time was short and if *they* came back, she needed to have shared the message.

The phone rang once. Twice. With a brrping sound it connected.

"Hello?" A male answered and she felt a warm flush of relief at the voice. A voice she knew well.

"The manor has been breached. The girl child taken." The words erupted and her hand trembled.

"On our way." The click of the receiver being replaced echoed loudly in the stillness of the room.

Copper. She smelled copper.

Her stomach soured, knowing it meant more deaths. Jemima looked around for the gun—a gun with deadly, holy water-infused copper bullets—she knew was hidden somewhere in the room. A gun she couldn't find. *No divine intervention exists here*, she thought.

Hopefully *they* didn't remain. Feeding. If they were still here, that's what they would be doing. She found a corner and scrunched down, hiding from sight.

Crouched low, she tried to stay as still as possible, listening for sounds of the vehicles she knew would be coming. She dug her fingers into the flesh of her arms; remaining aware enough to stop before drawing blood. That would surely bring them out. Jemima dragged the cloak around her to capture the warmth, yet there was little to be found.

The sounds of engines roused her from the corner of the room.

Jemima inched toward the window, the lead of the old glass distorting her view, hearing raised voices she knew Mistress Cressida had arrived.

Jemima retreated. Remained hidden from the woman because if she knew, all may well be lost. From the shadowed room she listened to the conversation...

"It smells like Estersham." The Mistress' eyes closed. "If it is, we have a problem." She turned once more, her face set and eyes now glacial in intensity. "James?"

The man nodded as if he knew what was to come.

"If I take those steps, I cannot return. Another must stand in my place." Her voice hardened while her eyes glittered in the dim light, piercing in their intensity.

Then the Mistress' voice called out in the near silence. "You and yours have been my loyal servants for so many years. I took an oath to protect you long ago. I renewed it with marriage and births, over and over. Now, my home and yours have been breached and this child taken from us. The girl child, who will be the hope and salvation of our kind, was ripped from the bosom of our nest. I will repay your loyalty and I will get her back." The words of power rippled in the night and licked at Jemima's skin.

Available in Ebook
books2read.com/BloodBride-Nix

Direct Autographed Copy
https://www.imogenenix.net/BloodBride

Also by Imogene Nix

Warriors of the Elector

- Star of Ishtar
- Starline
- Starfire
- Star of the Fleet
- Starburst
- The Star of Eternity

The Star of Ishtar & Starline - Print

Starfire & Star of the Fleet - Print

Starburst & The Star of Eternity - Print

Blood Secrets

- The Blood Bride
- The Illuminated Witch
- The Sorcerer's Touch

The Secrets World:

Blood Secrets

- The Blood Bride
- The Illuminated Witch
- The Sorcerer's Touch

House Secrets

- As Dawn Breaks

- Immortal Consequences
- Edge of Night

All That Glitters - a House Secrets Novella

Danu's Secrets

- The Downfall of Padraic O'Shaunessy
- Unnamed Secrets Book II

The Automaton Series

- Haven House
- Nobel Crest
- Casa Bonita

The Search Duology

- Miss Elspeth's Desire
- Miss Isabelle's Craving

Duology World Novels

- A Very Merry Widow

Reunion Trilogy

- War's End
- The Assassin
- Executing Justice

The Reunion Trilogy in Paperback

Sex Love & Aliens

- Tangled Webs

- False Webs
- Covert Webs

21st Testing Protocol

- Cyborg: Redux
- Children Of A Greater Evil
- When Evil Came To Stay
- Finis: The War To End All Wars

Celtic Cupid Trilogy

- Blame The Wine
- A Stranger's Embrace
- Revenge On Cupid

The Celtic Cupid Trilogy in Paperback

Zombieology

- The Reset
- I Dream of Zombies
- The Six Million Dollar Zombie
- Make Room For Zombies
- Days of Our Zombies
- Unnamed Zobiology title (coming soon)

Knights of Pleasure

- Silken Knights

Single Titles

The Chocolate Affair (also in Print)

Falling In Love Again (Previously A Sapphire For Karina)

BioCybe (also in Print)

Hesparia's Tears (also in Print)

Tomorrow's Promise

A Bar In Paris (also in Print)

Inheritance Of The Blood (also in Print)

The Plan

Loving Memories (also in Print)

Hero of Heartbreak Hill (also in Print)

My One & Only

Curse Bound

Non Fiction

Self Publishing: Absolute Beginners Guide (With Suzi Love)

Written as Ciara Cave

25 Curated Ways To Get Rid Of Telemarketers

Book Signings for Absolute Beginners

About the Author

Imogene is published in a range of romance genres including Paranormal, Science Fiction and Contemporary. She is mainly published in the UK and USA.

In 2010, Imogene Nix (the pen name not Imogene herself) was born. Imogene sat down and worked tirelessly for 3 months culminating in the book Starline, which became the first in a trilogy titled, "Warriors of the Elector." Since then she's had over 30 titles published and is now focusing on hybridising herself - with a mixture of traditionally published and self-published works.

In fact, she's taking control of many of her back catalogue books, which are slowly re-releasing as self-published titles.

Imogene is a member of a range of professional organisations world wide, and believes in the mantra of mentoring and paying it forward and is actively involved in mentorship (through NaNoWrimo and her vlog: In The Chair With Imogene Nix) and tutoring of new and upcoming authors.

In her spare time she loves to drink coffee, wine & eat chocolate and is parenting her spoiled dog and a ferocious cat along with her husband and daughter and looks forward to weekends away with her husband in their caravan "The Seven Year Hitch!" Do look forward to her caravan romance at some point!